Nick was acutely aware of the fact that he was crossing a line.

A line he had never ventured over before.

The man he'd evolved into would have never given in to the moment, to the temptation that was shimmering before him.

No matter how much he wanted to.

He cupped the sides of Georgie's face in his hands and brought his mouth down to hers as if he had no choice in the matter.

And it was that needy soul who silently cheered as sensation went shooting through him. He deepened the kiss that was as far from innocent as day was from night.

Dearest Reader,

Welcome to the first book of a brand-new, exciting
continuity, THE COLTONS: FAMILY FIRST. As always,
there's mystery, intrigue and, of course, romance. Set in
and around the small Texas town of Esperanza, forty
miles south of San Antonio, there is nothing small about
the emotions being played out here. In the first book we
meet Georgeann Grady Colton, Georgie to her friends,
a rodeo competitor who is also a young single mother,
determined to provide a stable home for her precocious little
girl, something Georgie and her two older brothers didn't
have when they were growing up. Fresh off a five-month
and hopefully final stint of following the rodeo circuit,
competing for purses that will allow her to finally settle
down, Georgie comes home only to have Secret Service
Agent Nick Sheffield literally burst into her life. It seems
that progressively more threatening e-mails are being sent
to presidential hopeful Senator Joe Colton. Nick has traced
their origin to Georgie's computer. Georgie proclaims her
innocence. At first Nick is highly skeptical, but he finally
believes her and the two strike up a wary partnership to find
out who has stolen Georgie's IP address, plus her identity
and her life as well. Along the route, two lonely people
allow the masks they show the world to slip and find not
only one another, but someone to love as well.

As ever, I thank you for reading, and from the bottom of my
heart, I wish you love.

Marie Ferrarella

MARIE FERRARELLA

Colton's Secret Service

Silhouette®
Romantic
SUSPENSE

Special thanks and acknowledgment to Marie Ferrarella
for her contribution to The Coltons:
Family First miniseries.

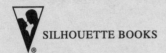 SILHOUETTE BOOKS

ISBN-13: 978-0-373-27598-4
ISBN-10:   0-373-27598-6

COLTON'S SECRET SERVICE

Visit Silhouette Books at www.eHarlequin.com

Printed in U.S.A.

Books by Marie Ferrarella

MARIE FERRARELLA

This *USA TODAY* bestselling and RITA® Award-winning author has written more than one hundred and fifty books for Silhouette, some under the name Marie Nicole. Her romances are beloved by fans worldwide. Visit her Web site at www.marieferrarella.com.

To
Patience Smith,
who makes being an author
such a pleasure

Chapter 1

His neck was really beginning to ache.

It amazed him how these last ten years, after steadily climbing up the ladder, from cop to detective to Secret Service agent, Nick Sheffield found himself right back where he started: doing grunt work. There was no other accurate way to describe it: remaining stationary, hour after hour, waiting for a perpetrator to finally show up— provided he did show up, which was never a sure thing.

But, at least for now, Nick had no other recourse, no other trail to pursue. This lonely ranch was where the evidence had led him.

He'd always hated surveillance work. Ever since he'd been a young kid, patience had never been in his nature. He was much happier being active. *Doing* something instead of just standing as still as a statue, feeling his five o'clock shadow grow.

However, in this particular instance, it was unavoidably necessary. He had no other way to capture his quarry.

Nick supposed he should consider this a triumph. After all, less than twenty-four hours ago, he still hadn't a clue where all those threatening letters and e-mails aimed at the man whose life he was to safeguard, Senator Joe Colton, came from. These days, it seemed like every crazy malcontent and his dog had access to a computer and the Internet, which made tracking down the right crazy malcontent one hell of a challenge. One that fortunately, he was more than up to—with a healthy dose of help from the reformed computer hacker, Steve Hennessey, who now worked for his security staff.

Technically, it was the Senator's staff, but he ran it. Handpicked the people and ran the staff like a well-oiled, efficient machine ever since he'd been assigned to the Senator. He liked to think that he was doing his bit to help the Senator get elected to the highest post of the land.

There was no doubt in his mind that unless something unforeseen or drastic happened, the Senator would go on to become the next President of the United States. In his opinion, and he'd been around more than a little in his thirty years on earth, there was no other man even half as qualified to assume the position of President as Senator Joe Colton.

He didn't just work for the Senator, he admired the man, admired what he stood for and what he hoped to accomplish once elected. In the last few months, he'd seen Senator Colton up close and under less-than-favorable conditions. In his opinion, they just did not come any more genuine—or charismatic—than the Senator.

Nick doubted very much if he would have spent the

last eight hours standing behind a slightly open barn door, watching the front of an unoccupied, ramshackle ranch house for anyone else.

Damn it, where the hell was this creep? Was he going to show at all?

He didn't want to have to do this for another hour, much less entertain the prospect of doing it for another day.

Nick's temper was getting frayed. It was late and humid, and the mosquitoes kept trying to make a meal out of him. He waved another one away from his neck even as he felt sweat sliding down his spine, making the shirt beneath his black jacket stick to his skin. Talk about discomfort.

Nick blew out a frustrated breath.

Why couldn't this crazy be located in one of the major cities, living in a high-rise apartment? Why did it have to be someone who lived the life of a hermit? The IP address that Steve had miraculously tracked down had brought him to a town that barely made the map. A blip of a town named Esperanza, Texas.

Esperanza. Now there was a misnomer. His Spanish wasn't all that good, but he knew that *esperanza* was the Spanish word for "hope" and in this particular case, Nick had no doubt that the hope associated with the town was reserved for those who managed to escape from it. If it wasn't for the fact that Esperanza was a sub-suburb of San Antonio, Nick doubted that he and his GPS system would have been able to even locate it.

And this person he was after didn't even reside within the so-called city limits. He lived in an old, all-but-falling-down ranch house that stood five miles from the nearest neighbor, and was even farther away than five miles from the town.

Hell, Nick thought impatiently, this character could be cooking up bombs and nobody would ever be the wiser—until the explosion came.

Nobody but him, Nick thought. But that was his job, tracking down the crazies and keeping them away from the best man he'd met in a long, long time.

"You're sure?" the Senator had asked him when he'd walked into his office with the news yesterday that his hacker had finally managed to isolate where the e-mails originated. He'd quickly given him the exact location.

For the most part, Nick didn't even bother telling the Senator about the nuisance calls, e-mails and letters that had found their way into the campaign headquarters. Anyone in public office, or even the public eye, was a target for someone seeking to vent his or her discontent. It came with the territory.

But this was different. These e-mails and letters smacked of someone dangerous. Someone seeking to "take you out" as one of the last ranting communications had threatened.

Nick had learned a long time ago to take seriously anything that remotely resembled a threat. The risk was too great not to.

He'd just informed the Senator that the sender was someone living in or around Esperanza, Texas, and that he intended to confront the man face-to-face. It was against the law to threaten a presidential candidate.

"That it's coming from there?" Nick asked, then went ahead as if he'd received a positive response. "I wouldn't be coming to you with this if I wasn't sure," he told the Senator simply.

Between them, on the desk, was a thick pile of papers

that Nick had emptied out of a manila folder. Letters that had arrived in the last few weeks, all from the same source. All progressively angrier in nature. It couldn't be ignored any longer, even if he were so inclined.

"We've tracked him down," Nick repeated. "And, unless you have something specific that only I can take care of here, I'd like to go down to this little two-bit hick place and make sure that this nut-job doesn't decide to follow through with any of his threats." He had no qualms about leaving the Senator. He was the head of the Secret Service detail, but by no means was he the only one assigned to the popular Senator. Hathaway and Davis were more than up to watching over the man until he got back.

"These are all from him?" Nick nodded in response to the Senator's question. "Sure has spent a lot of time venting," Joe commented. He picked up a sheet of paper only to have Nick stop him before he was able to begin to read it.

"No need to read any of it, Senator." Nick wanted to spare the man the ugliness on some of the pages. "It's pretty awful."

Joe didn't believe in isolating himself, but he saw no reason to immerse himself in distasteful lies and name-calling, either. He let the letter remain in Nick's hand. "Then why did you bring it to me?"

In Nick's opinion, the volume of mail spoke for itself. No sane person invested this much time and effort in sending vicious missives, and the future actions of an insane person couldn't be safely gauged. It would take very little to push a person like this to where he would become dangerous.

"To let you see that the man could be a threat and that

I'd like the chance to stop him before he becomes one," Nick stated simply.

In the short time they had been together, Joe had learned to both like and rely on the head of his Secret service detail. Nick Sheffield had impressed him as a hard-working, honorable man whose interest was in getting the job done, not in gathering attention or praise for his actions. He more than trusted the man's instincts.

Joe liked the fact that Nick always looked him in the eye when he spoke. "When would you leave?" he asked.

"Tonight." Nick saw a glint of surprise in the Senator's eyes. "I should be back in a couple of days— a week at most," he promised, although he was hoping that it wouldn't take that long. He intended to locate the sender, take him into custody and bring him back. The federal authorities could take it from there.

Joe nodded. There had been mutual respect between the two men almost from the very first day. Their personalities complemented one another. Joe trusted Nick not only with his life, but, more importantly, the lives of his family who meant more to him than anything else in the world, including the bid for the presidency.

"All right," the Senator agreed. "Go if you really think it's necessary."

There was no hesitation on Nick's part. "I do."

"That's good enough for me," the Senator replied. And then he smiled that smile that had a way of cutting across party affiliations and verbose rhetoric, burrowing into the heart of the recipient. "Just get back as soon as you can, Nick. I feel a whole lot better knowing that you're on the job."

Nick knew the man was not just giving voice to empty words, that praise from the Senator was always heartfelt and genuine. While exceedingly charming, with a manner that drew people to him, the Senator was not one to toss around words without thought or feeling behind them, like so many other politicians.

"I'll be back before you know it," Nick had promised, taking his leave. At the time, he sincerely meant what he said.

Georgeann Grady, Georgie to everyone who knew her, struggled mightily to keep her eyes open. For the last twenty minutes, she'd debated pulling over to the side of the road in order to catch a few well-deserved winks before falling asleep at the wheel. But she was only five miles away from home. Five miles away from sleeping in her own bed and after months of being on the road, sleeping in her own bed sounded awfully good to her.

She told herself to keep driving.

Digging her nails into the palms of the hands that were wrapped around the steering wheel of her truck, Georgie tried to shake off the effects of sleepiness by tossing her head. It sent the single thick, red braid back over her shoulder. Squaring them, she glanced into the rear-view mirror to check on her pint-sized passenger.

Big, wide green eyes looked right back at her.

Georgie suppressed a sigh. She might have known that Emmie wasn't asleep, even if her nonstop chatter had finally run its course. Ceasing about ten minutes ago.

"Why aren't you asleep?" she asked her precocious, almost-five-year-old daughter.

"Too excited," Emmie told her solemnly in a voice that could have easily belonged to someone at least twice her age.

Emmie sounded almost happier to be getting back home than she was. Sometimes, Georgie thought, it was almost as if their roles were reversed and Emmie was the mother while she was the daughter. There was little more than eighteen years between them. They could have just as easily been sisters instead of mother and daughter.

And, as far as daughters went, she couldn't have asked for a better one. Raising Emmie had been a dream, despite the unorthodox life they led. A good deal of Emmie's life had been spent on the road, as a rodeo brat. It was out of necessity so that Georgie could earn money by competing in various rodeo events—just as her mother and her grandfather had before her.

At all times, her eye was on the prize. The final prize. Not winning some title that would be forgotten by the time the dust settled, but amassing as much money as she could so that she and her daughter could finally settle down and live a normal life.

She owed it to Emmie.

Her mother, Mary Lynn Grady, had quit the life, walking away with nothing more than medals and trophies, as she took up the reins of motherhood. But she intended to be far more prepared than that. It took money to make dreams come true.

Emmie was coming of age. She'd be turning five next week and five meant kindergarten, which in turn meant stability. That translated into living in a home that wasn't on wheels, nestled in a place around people who loved her. That had been the plan for the last four-something years and Georgie was determined to make it a reality.

Every cent that hadn't been used for clothing and feeding them, or for entrance fees, had faithfully been banked back in Esperanza. By her tally, at this point, thanks to her most recent winning streak, the account was exceedingly healthy now. There was finally more than enough for them to settle down and for her to figure out her next move: finding a career that didn't involve performing tricks on a horse that was galloping at break-neck speed.

Any other career would seem tame in comparison, but right now, tame was looking awfully good. The accident that she'd had a few months ago could have been disastrous. It made her very aware that she, like so many other rodeo competitors, was living on borrowed time. She wanted to get out before time ran out on her—and now, she could.

Independence had a wonderful feel about it, she thought.

Emmie's unbridled excitement about coming home just underscored her decision. There'd be no pulling over to the side of the road for her. Not when they were almost home.

Leaning forward, Georgie turned up the music. Tobey Keith's newest song filled the inside of the cab. Behind her, in an enthusiastic, clear voice, Emmie began to sing along. With a laugh, Georgie joined in.

In the overall scheme of things, eight hours was nothing, but when those hours peeled away, second by second, moment by moment, it felt as if the time was endless.

He wanted to get back to the action, not feel as if his limbs were slowly slipping into paralysis. But he didn't even dare get back to the car he'd hidden behind the barn. He might miss his quarry coming home. The man *had* to come home sometime. The e-mails had been coming fairly regularly, one or more almost every day now. Because there hadn't been anything yesterday, the man was overdue.

Nick took out a candy bar he'd absently shoved into his pocket last night. It was just before leaving Prosperino, California, the Senator's home base, to catch the red-eye flight to San Antonio. After checking in with his team to see if there were any further developments—there hadn't been—he'd rented a car and then driven to this god-forsaken piece of property.

He'd found the front door unlocked and had let himself in, but while there were some signs here and there that the ranch house was lived in, the place had been empty.

So he'd set up surveillance. And here he'd been for the last interminable eight hours, fifteen minutes and God only knew how many seconds, waiting.

It would be nice, he thought irritably, if this character actually showed up soon so he could wrap this all up and go back to civilization before he started growing roots where he stood.

How the hell did people live in places like this? he wondered. If the moon hadn't been full tonight, he wouldn't even be able to *see* the house from here, much less the front door. Most likely, he'd probably have to crouch somewhere around the perimeter of the building as he laid in wait.

He supposed that things could always be worse.

Stripping the wrapper off a large-sized concoction of chocolate, peanuts and caramel, Nick had just taken his first bite of the candy bar when he heard it. A rumbling engine noise.

Nick froze, listening.

It was definitely a car. From the sound of it, not a small one. Or a particularly new one for that matter.

Damn, but it was noisy enough to wake the dead, he thought. Whoever it was certainly wasn't trying for stealth, but then, the driver had no reason to expect anyone to be around for his entrance.

Because he was pretty close to starving before he remembered the candy bar, Nick took one more large bite, then shoved the remainder into his pocket.

All his senses were instantly on high alert.

He strained his eyes, trying to make out the approaching vehicle from his very limited vantage point. He didn't dare open the door any wider, at least, not at this point. He couldn't take a chance on the driver seeing the movement.

It suddenly occurred to him that if the driver decided to park his truck behind the barn, he was going to be out of luck. That was where he'd left his sedan.

Nick mentally crossed his fingers as he held his breath.

The next moment, he exhaled. Well, at least one thing was going right, he silently congratulated himself. The vehicle, an old, battered truck, came into view and was apparently going to park in front of the ranch house.

A minute later, he saw why the truck's progress was so slow. The truck was towing an equally ancient trailer.

As he squinted for a better view, Nick tried to make out the driver, but there was no way he could see into the cab. He couldn't tell if the man was young or old. The vague shadow he saw told him that the driver appeared to be slight and even that might have just been a trick of the moonlight.

Nick straightened his back, his ache miraculously gone. At least the ordeal was almost over, he told himself.

The truck finally came to a creaking stop before the ranch house, but not before emitting a cacophony. It almost sounded as if it exhaled. Straining his eyes, Nick still heard rather than saw the driver getting out of the truck's cab.

Now or never, Nick thought.

"Stop right there," he shouted, bursting out of the barn. He held up his wallet, opened to his ID. As if anyone could make out what was there, he thought ironically. To cover all bases, he identified himself loudly. "I'm with the Secret Service."

In response, the driver turned and bolted back toward the truck.

"Oh, no, you don't," Nick shouted.

A star on his high school track team, Nick took off, cutting the distance between them down to nothing in less than a heartbeat. The next moment, he tackled the driver, bringing him down.

"Get the hell off me!" the driver shouted.

Nick remembered thinking that the truck driver had a hell of a feminine voice just before he felt the back of his head explode, ushering in a curtain of darkness.

Chapter 2

It was only through sheer grit that Nick managed to hang on to the fringes of consciousness, gripping the sliver of light with his fingertips and holding on for all he was worth. He knew that if he surrendered to the darkness, there would be no telling what could happen. In his experience these last ten years, death could be hiding behind every conceivable corner. Even in tiny, off-the-beaten-path burgs that made no one's top-ten list of places to visit.

Falling backward, Nick teetered, then managed to spring up, somehow still miraculously holding on to his wallet and displaying both his badge and ID.

Not that anyone was looking at it.

"Striking a Secret Service agent is a punishable offense that'll land you in prison," he barked at his assailant.

Swinging around to face the person who'd almost

bashed in his head, Nick struggled to focus. Everything appeared blurred, with images multiplying themselves. This intense ringing in his ears jarred him down to the very bone. But even though it was wavy, the image of his assailant was legions away from what he had expected.

Was he hallucinating?

There, standing with her legs spread apart and firmly planted on the ground, clutching a tire iron that was close to being half as big as she was, was—

"A kid?" Nick demanded incredulously when he could finally find his voice. "I was almost brained by a little kid?"

"I'm not little! And you stay off my mama!" the tiny terror shouted. She held on to the tire iron so hard, her knuckles were white and she'd lifted her chin like a pint-sized, old-fashioned prize fighter, daring him to try to touch her.

His head throbbed and the headache mushrooming over his skull threatened to obliterate everything else.

Focus, Nick, focus!

"Your mama?" Nick echoed. Well, that explained it all right. His ears hadn't been playing tricks on him. The driver he'd tackled had sounded like a woman for a very good reason. "He" was a "she."

Even as he fought to clear his brain and try to keep the headache at bay, he saw the woman—and now that he looked, he could see that she was a petite, curvaceous woman whose body could *not* be mistaken for boyish—move swiftly to stand beside her daughter. She rested her hand on one of the little girl's shoulders. The woman had lost the ridiculous, oversized cowboy hat she'd had on. Without it, he saw that she had red hair. It was pulled back and tucked into a long, thick braid that ran down to the small of her back.

The fiery-looking, petite hellcat didn't look as if she could weigh a hundred pounds even with her daughter perched on her shoulders. He should have easily subdued both of them with no trouble, not find himself at their mercy.

This wasn't going to look good in the report.

The woman took the tire iron from her daughter. But rather than drop it, the way he expected her to, she grasped it like a weapon while gently attempting to push the little hellion behind her. The girl didn't stay put long. It reminded Nick of a painting he'd once seen in a Washington museum, something that had to do with the spirit of the pioneer women who helped settle the West.

For one unguarded moment, between the monumental headache, the intermittent confusion and the anger he felt at being caught off guard like this, the word *magnificent* came to mind.

The next moment, he realized this was no time for that kind of personal assessment.

He found himself under fire from that rather pert set of lips.

"Who the hell are you?" she demanded hotly, moving the tire iron as she shot off the words. "And what are you doing, sneaking around on my land, attacking defenseless women?"

"I already told you who I was," he reminded her tersely, "and I'd hardly call you defenseless."

As he said that, he rubbed his chin and realized belatedly that the woman he'd inadvertently tackled had actually landed a rather stinging right cross to his chin.

Maybe he was damn lucky to be alive, although he probably wouldn't feel quite that way if word of this incident ever really got out: Nick Sheffield, aspiring Secret Service agent to the President, taken down by two females who collectively weighed less than a well-fed male German shepherd.

He eyed the tire iron in her hand. "I feel sorry for your husband."

"Don't be," Georgie snapped. "There isn't one."

Once upon a time, during the summer that she'd been seventeen and full of wonderful, naive dreams, she'd wanted a home, a husband, a family, the whole nine yards. And, equally naively, she'd thought that Jason Prentiss was the answer to all her prayers. Tall, intelligent and handsome, the Dartmouth College junior was spending the summer on his uncle's farm. She'd lost her heart the first moment she'd seen him. He had eyes the color of heaven and a tongue that was dipped in honey.

Unfortunately, he also possessed a heart that was chiseled out of old bedrock. Once summer was over, he went back to college, back, she discovered, to his girlfriend. Finding out that their summer romance had created a third party only made Jason pack his bags that much faster. He left with a vague promise to write and quickly vanished from her life. In the months that followed, there wasn't a single attempt to contact her. The two letters she wrote were returned, unopened.

Georgie had grown up in a hurry that summer, in more ways than one. Eighteen was a hell of an age to become an adult, but she had and in her opinion, she and Emmie were just fine—barring the occasional bump in the road.

Like the one standing in front of her now.

Sucking in his breath against the pain, Nick rubbed the back of his head where Emmie had made more than gentle contact.

It was a wonder she hadn't fractured his skull, he thought. As it was, there would be one hell of a lump there. Probing, he could feel it starting to form.

No husband, huh? "Killed him, did you?" he asked sarcastically.

He saw the woman's eyes flash like green lightning. Obviously, he'd struck a nerve. Had she really killed her husband?

"I don't know what you're doing here, but I want you to turn around and get the hell off my property or I'm going to call the sheriff," she warned.

Nick held his ground even as he eyed the little devil the woman was vainly trying to keep behind her. He was more leery of the kid than the woman. The little girl looked as if she would bite.

"Call away," he told the woman, unfazed. He saw that his answer annoyed her and he felt as if he'd scored a point for his side. "It'll save me the trouble of looking up his number."

"Right." She drew the word out, indicating that she didn't come close to believing him. Inclining her head slightly toward her daughter, she nonetheless kept her eyes trained on him. "Emmie, get my cell phone out of the truck." Her eyes hardened as she turned her full attention back to him. "We don't like people who trespass around here."

Okay, he'd had just about enough of this grade B western clone.

"Look, I already told you that I'm a Secret Service agent—" Nick got no farther.

Georgie snorted contemptuously at what she perceived to be a whopper. Anyone could get a badge off the Internet and fake an ID these days. "And I'm Annie Oakley."

"Well, *Ms. Oakley,*" Nick retorted sarcastically, "right now, you're interfering with a federal matter."

When it came to sarcasm, she could hold her own with the best of them. Growing up with no father and her lineage in question, the butt of more than one joke, she'd learned quickly to use the tools she had to deflect the hurtful words.

"And just what matter would that be?" she asked.

Although he rarely justified himself, he decided to give this woman the benefit of the doubt. Maybe she wasn't playing dumb, maybe the more-than-mildly attractive hellcat really *was* dumb.

So he spelled it out for her. "Obstruction of justice, harboring a criminal—"

She stopped him cold. "What criminal?" Georgie demanded angrily.

This man was *really* getting under her skin. God, but she wished she had her shotgun with her instead of this hunk of metal. Wielding a tire iron didn't make her feel very safe.

"Georgie Grady," he answered. He had his doubts that she was innocent of the man's activities. Not if she lived here as she claimed. Even so, Nick decided to cover his bases and give reasoning a try. "Look, your boyfriend or whoever Georgie Grady is to you is in a lot of trouble and if you try to hide him, it'll only go hard on you as well." Needing some kind of leverage, he hit her where he assumed it would hurt the most. "Do you want Social Services to take away your daughter?"

He nodded at the returning child holding on to the cell phone she'd been sent to get. "I can make that happen."

"Can you, now?" He was bluffing, Georgie thought. The man didn't know his ass from his elbow, he'd just proven it. "Somehow, that doesn't fill me full of fear," she informed him coldly.

"Mama?"

There was fear in Emmie's voice. Georgie's protective mother instincts immediately stood at attention. She slipped one arm around her daughter's small shoulders to give her a quick, comforting squeeze.

"But someone upsetting my daughter does fill me full of anger and I promise you, mister, when I'm angry, it's not a pretty sight." Her eyes became glinting, green slits as she narrowed them. "You'd do well to avoid it if you can."

What the hell was he doing, standing in the middle of nowhere, going one-on-one with some misguided red-headed harpy? He'd had enough of this. "Just tell me where I can find this Georgie Grady and I'll forget this whole incident."

Emmie tugged on the bottom of her mother's shirt to get her attention. "Is he simple, Mama?" she asked in what amounted to a stage whisper.

Georgie stifled a laugh. "It would appear so, honey."

He was not here to entertain them, nor did he appreciate being the butt of someone's joke, especially when he wasn't in on it. "Look, call the damn sheriff so we can get this over with."

To his surprise, she took a step toward him, lifting her chin exactly the way he'd seen her daughter do. "I will thank you not to use profanity in front of my daughter."

Of all the hypocritical— "But you just cursed," he pointed out.

Georgie allowed a careless shrug to roll off her shoulders. "That's different."

Of course it was. "God, but I hate small towns."

"And using the Lord's name in vain's pretty much frowned on around here as well," Georgie told him, not bothering to hide her disdain.

Well, it was obvious that no matter what she said, she wasn't calling the sheriff and he wanted this thing brought to a conclusion. "Fine, tell me the sheriff's number." He began to reach into his suit jacket pocket. "*I'll* call him and we can get this over with."

Alarmed that he might be reaching for a concealed weapon, Georgie raised the tire iron threateningly. "Put your hands up!" she ordered.

Abandoning his cell phone, Nick did as she said. "I can't dial and put my hands up," he protested. He was miles beyond annoyed now.

The woman seemed to relax, lowering the tire iron again. She raised her eyes to his and he could have sworn he saw a smirk. Her next words did nothing to dispel that impression.

"Don't do your research very well, do you, Mr. Secret Service agent?"

No matter how he focused, he hadn't a clue what she was driving at and he was very tired of these mind games. She was undoubtedly stalling for time. If he didn't know better, he would have said she was trying to give her boyfriend time to escape—except that he already knew the man wasn't in the ranch house.

"What are you talking about?" he asked.

She debated stringing him along for a bit, then

decided that more than wanting to get to him, she wanted him *gone*. There was only one way that was going to happen. "Well, for one thing, Mr. phony Secret Service agent—" she'd seen more convincing IDs in Howard Beasley's Toy Emporium "—*I'm* Georgie Grady."

"No, you're not." If ever he'd seen someone who *didn't* look like a "Georgie" it was this woman in the tight, faded jeans and the checkered work shirt that seemed to be sticking to every inch of her upper torso like a second skin, thanks to the humidity.

Georgie shook her head. Talk about a blockhead. Too bad he was so damn annoying, because, all things considered, he was kind of cute—as long as he lost the black suit and stopped using so much of that styling goop on his hair.

"Then the people who put that name on the trophy I just won at the last rodeo competition are going to feel pretty stupid," she told him.

Nick had to consciously keep his jaw from dropping. He eyed her incredulously. This was just outlandish enough to be true. "*You're* Georgie Grady."

"I'm Georgie Grady. I guess you've got a hearing problem as well as lacking any manners," she surmised. She looked down at her daughter. "Gotta feel sorry for a man like that, Emmie. He doesn't know any better."

He was hot, he was tired and his head was splitting. He was in no mood to be talked about as if he wasn't standing right there. Especially by his quarry if this woman really was Georgie Grady.

"Look," he said waspishly, "this is all very entertaining, but I don't have time for an episode of *The Waltons*—"

The woman watched him blankly. It was obvious that the title of the popular classic TV show meant nothing to her. "Must've been before my time," she commented. She nodded over his shoulder. "The road's that way. I suggest you take it."

She still had him holding his hands up. "Can I put my hands down?"

She pretended to think his question over. "Only after you start walking."

"Fair enough."

As if complying, Nick turned away from her, took two steps, dropped his hands and then turned around again. This time, instead of his ID, he had his service revolver in his hand.

And he was pointing it at the woman.

Startled, Georgie took a firmer grip on the tire iron. Seeing the gun, Emmie screamed and this time, the little girl allowed herself to be pushed behind her mother's back.

"Drop the tire iron," Nick ordered. His tone brooked no nonsense. "Now!" he barked when she didn't immediately comply.

Letting the tire iron fall, Georgie bit off a curse that would have curled the hair of the most hardened bronco buster had it made it past her lips. She should have known this was all a ruse. Served her right for taking pity on him because he was cute. When was she going to learn that cute men meant nothing but trouble in the long *and* short run?

"I don't have anything worth stealing," she told him between clenched teeth. She just wanted him gone. He was scaring Emmie and for that, she wanted to rip out his heart.

Nick took a step closer. Although small, the gun felt heavy in his hand. He didn't like pulling his weapon on a woman and even though he found the child annoying, he definitely didn't care for having to train a weapon around the little girl, but the firebrand who claimed to be her mother had left him no choice.

"As I was saying," he went on as if nothing had happened, "I'm here to arrest Georgie Grady and take him—or her—into custody. Put your hands up," he told her.

Georgie raised her hands. Out of the corner of her eye, she saw Emmie mimic her action.

You'll pay for this, mister, she silently promised. Her brain worked feverishly to figure a way out of this.

"So," Georgie began slowly, "you really are a Secret Service agent."

"That's what I told you."

Georgie nodded her head, as if finally believing him. "And why would a Secret Service agent want to take me into custody?" she queried, doing her best to hang on to her temper. He had the gun, shouting at him wouldn't be advisable.

"Mama, is he going to shoot you?" Emmie cried, suddenly sounding like every one of her four years and no more.

Georgie's heart almost broke. Barely holding up her hands, she bent down to Emmie's level.

"No, honey, he's not going to shoot me. He's not that dumb," she assured her daughter. Raising her eyes to his, she sought his back up. "Are you, Mr. Secret Service agent?"

He'd only discharged his weapon three times, and never in his present position. But saying so might sound weak to the woman. Who knew how these backwoods people thought?

"Not if you cooperate."

She rose to her feet again, but this time she wasn't holding up her hands. She was holding Emmie in her arms, determined to calm the child's fears despite the fact that beneath her own anger was a solid band of fear. She had no idea who this crazy person was, only that she doubted very much that he was who he claimed to be. Secret Service agents didn't come to places like Esperanza.

She wished now that she'd stopped at her brother's place instead of coming here tonight. Clay's ranch wasn't home, but it did have electricity, something her house didn't at the moment because she'd shut it off before she'd gone on the trail. And more importantly, Clay's place didn't have someone holding a dingy looking revolver that was pointed straight at her.

She shifted her body so that she was between the gun and Emmie. "And just how do you expect me to 'cooperate'?" she asked.

"By letting me take you into custody." He began to feel as if he was trapped in some sort of time loop, endlessly repeating the same words.

He'd already said that, and it was just as ridiculous now as when he'd first said it. "Why, for God's sakes?" she demanded.

"I thought you didn't believe in taking the Lord's name in vain," Nick mocked, throwing her words back at her.

"It's okay when I do it," she informed him coolly, tossing her head in a dismissive movement. "God likes me. I don't point guns at little girls."

Damn, how the hell did this woman manage to keep

putting him on the defensive? She was the criminal here, not him.

"I'm pointing the gun at you, not her." He saw the little girl thread her arms around the woman's neck in what could only be seen as a protective action. They were some pair, these two. "And I'm doing it because you left me no choice."

All right, she'd played along long enough. She wanted answers now. "What is it that I'm supposed to have done that has gotten your Secret Service agent shorts all twisted up in a knot?" she demanded.

She knew damn well what she'd done. He had the utmost faith that the hacker on his team had given him the right information. Steve'd had one hell of a reputation before he'd gotten caught.

"Don't act so innocent," he accused.

"Sorry," she retorted sarcastically, "but it's a habit I have when I haven't done anything wrong."

"I wouldn't call sending threatening letters to Senator Colton not doing anything wrong," Nick informed her.

Georgie felt as if someone had just hit her over the head with a nine-pound skillet. "Senator Colton?" she echoed.

He saw the look of recognition flash in her eyes. She'd just given herself away. He was right. She *was* the one sending the threatening letters. The innocent act was just that, an act. While he felt vindicated, the slightest ribbon of disappointment weaved through him. He had no idea why, but chalked it up to the blow on the head he'd received.

"Yes."

"Senator *Joe* Colton?" Georgie enunciated in disbelief.

Why was she belaboring this? What was she up to? He wondered suspiciously, never taking his eyes off her face. "Yes."

"Well, that cinches it," Georgie said with finality, unconsciously hugging Emmie closer to her. "You really *are* out of your mind."

Chapter 3

Nick bristled at the insult. "My state of mind isn't in question here."

It was on the tip of her tongue to tell him that he was crazy if he thought she would have anything to do with another Colton after her mother's experience. But that would lead to questions she didn't want to answer. "And mine is?"

His eyes met hers. "You're the one sending the threatening e-mails."

If she weren't holding Emmie, she would have thrown up her hands. "*What* threatening e-mails? I've been too damn busy working to pick up a phone, much less waste my time on the computer."

When she came right down to it, Georgie didn't care for the Internet. To her, it was just another way for people to lose the human touch and slip into a vague pea soup of anonymity. The only reason she kept a computer and maintained an Internet account was because she didn't want to fall behind the rest of the world. Once Emmie started going to school, she knew that a computer would be a necessity. In no time at all, she was certain computers would take the place of loose-leaf binders, notebooks and textbooks. She wanted to be able to help her daughter, not have Emmie ashamed of her because she was electronically challenged.

But that didn't mean she had to like the damn thing.

Her protests fell on deaf ears. The venom he'd seen spewed in those latest e-mails wouldn't have taken much time to fire off. She hadn't even bothered with spell-check, as he recalled. And the grammar in some of the messages had been pretty bad.

"My tech expert tracked it to your ranch house, your IP account."

She had no idea what an IP account was, but wasn't about to display her ignorance, especially not in front of her daughter. But she did know one thing. "Your tech expert is wrong."

"He's never wrong." It was both the best and the worst thing about Steve because his results could never be challenged.

Georgie was unmoved and unintimidated. With her mother the butt of narrow-minded people's jokes because all three of her children had been fathered by a man who was married to someone else, she'd had to stand up for herself at a very early age. That tended to either make or break a person. She'd always refused to be broken.

"Well, he just broke his streak because he *is* wrong and if the messages were traced to my ranch house, he's *doubly* wrong because I haven't *been* in my ranch house for the last five months."

Something told him that he should have investigated Georgie Grady a little before catching the red-eye to San Antonio, but time had been at a premium last night and he'd wanted to wrap this up fast.

His eyes swept over her. "Is that so?"

She rocked forward on the balls of her boot-shod feet. "Yes, that's 'so,' and I resent your attitude, you manner *and* your manhandling me."

"Lady, you got in a right cross and your daughter almost cracked open my skull with that tire iron of hers. If anyone was manhandled, it was me."

He saw a grin spread over otherwise pretty appealing lips. "Is that why you're so angry? Because you were bested by a woman a foot shorter than you and her four-year-old daughter?"

Not only was she cocky, but she wasn't observant either.

"You're not a foot shorter than me, more like eight inches," he estimated. "And I'm angry because I'm here in this one-horse town, wasting my time arguing with a pig-headed woman after waiting for the last eight hours for her to show up when I should be back in California, with the Senator."

"Well, go." Tucking Emmie against her hip, she waved him on his way with her temporarily free hand. "Nobody told you to come to Esperanza and harass innocent people."

Nick rolled his eyes. "This isn't getting us anywhere."

"Finally, we agree on something." She blew out a breath. One of them would have to be the voice of reason and because he didn't know the meaning of the word, it would have to be her. "You really a Secret Service Agent?"

"Yes."

"Can I see that ID again?"

Reaching into his pocket, he took out his wallet. "Not very trusting, are you?" He'd always thought that people in a small town were supposed to be incredibly trusting, to the point of almost being simple-minded. Him, he trusted no one. When you grow up, not being able to trust your own parents, it set a precedent.

She raised her eyes to his. "Should I be?" He was a stranger, for all she knew, he could be some serial killer, making the rounds.

His eyes slid over her. Someone as attractive as this woman needed to be on her guard more than most. That body of hers could get her in a great deal of trouble.

"No, I guess not." Opening his wallet to his badge and photo ID, he held it up for her to look over again.

Still keeping Emmie on her hip, Georgie leaned slightly in to peruse at length the ID he showed her.

As did Emmie. She stared at it so intently that Nick caught himself wondering if the annoying child could read. Wasn't she too young for that?

Georgie stepped back and looked at him with an air of resignation. The ID appeared to be authentic after all.

"I guess you are what you say you are." He felt her eyes slide over him. "You've got the black suit and those shades hanging out of your top pocket and all." There was that smirk again, he thought. The way she described him made him feel like a caricature. "And your hair's kind of slicked back, the part that's not messed up," she added.

Without realizing what he was doing, Nick ran his hand through his hair, smoothing down the section where the kid had hit him.

He saw the woman shake her head. "You'd look better with it all messed up. The other way looks like it's been glued down."

He knew what she was doing. She was trying to undermine him any way she could. Well, it wasn't going to work.

"We'll trade hairstyling tips some other time," he told her sarcastically.

Rather than put her in her place, his response seemed to amuse her.

"Touchy son of a gun, aren't you? Don't take criticism well, I see," she noted, as if to herself. She cocked her head, as if taking measure of him and trying to decide some things about him. You'd think he was the one in trouble, he thought, annoyed.

"You the one they used to make fun of when you were a kid?" she asked.

The exact opposite was true. He'd been more than half on his way to becoming a bully, threatening other kids at school. Smaller, bigger, it didn't matter, he took them all on because he could. In school and on the streets, at least some things were in his control. Not like at home where an abusive father made his life, and his alcohol-anesthetized mother's life, a living hell.

But then, one day, for reasons he had yet to completely understand, he suddenly saw himself through his victim's eyes. Saw his father as Drake Sheffield must have been at his age. Sickened, Nick released the kid who'd come within a hair's breadth of being pummeled to the ground because he'd mouthed off at him and just walked away.

After that, his life had turned around and he put himself on the path of protecting the underdog rather than trying to humiliate and take advantage of him.

"Well, were you?" Georgie queried, although, she couldn't quite see him as a classic ninety-eight-pound weakling.

"No" was all Nick said.

Her arms began to ache, reminding her that until this man had jumped out of the shadows, tackling her and causing her adrenaline to register off the charts, she'd been dead tired. It was getting really late.

Georgie decided to appeal to his sense of decency— if he had any. "Look, would you mind if I put my daughter to bed? It's been one back-breaking long day."

"I'm not tired," Emmie protested.

It was obvious that she didn't want to miss a second of what was going on. Because of the life she led, a child thrust into a world populated predominately by adults, Emmie thought like a miniature adult. Georgie was positive that if she'd elected to remain on the rodeo circuit, Emmie would have been thrilled to death. The little girl would have loved nothing better than to live in the run-down trailer amid her beloved cowboys forever. Especially because so many of them doted on her.

"That's okay," Georgie told her, "I am, pumpkin."

Emmie pulled her small features into a solemn expression. "Then you go to bed," the little girl advised her.

Georgie glanced at the dark-haired stranger. Yes, she was exhausted, but she was also agitated. There was no way she could have closed her eyes with this man around.

"Not hardly." She raised her eyebrows, silently indicating that she was still waiting for him to respond to her question. She didn't expect him to say no.

Nick gestured toward the door. "Go ahead."

Setting Emmie down, Georgie fished her house key out of her front pocket.

As she raised it to the keyhole, he said, "It's not locked."

She looked at him accusingly. Secret Service Agent or not, the man had some nerve. "You broke in?"

"No," Nick corrected patiently, "I found it unlocked."

The hell he did, she thought. "I locked up before I left," she informed him. In her absence, no one would have broken in. Everyone around here knew she had nothing worth stealing. He *had* to have been the one jimmying open her lock. How dumb did he think she was?

Pushing the door open, Georgie took Emmie's hand in hers and walked inside.

Nick followed in her wake. "Aren't you going to turn on the light?" he asked when she walked right by the switch at the front door.

"No light to turn on," she answered. The shadows in the room began to lengthen, swallowing up the pools of moonlight on the floor. She turned to see he was automatically closing the front door. "Keep the door open until I get the fire going," she instructed. Georgie quickly crossed to the fireplace.

Obliging her, Nick pushed the door opened again. He saw her squatting down in front of the fireplace, bunching up newspapers and sticking them strategically between the logs.

"In case you haven't noticed, it's June," he protested. A damn sticky June at that. "Isn't it too hot for a fire?"

"Not if you want coffee."

Finished, she glanced over her shoulder at him. The Secret Service agent was still standing in the doorway. The moonlight outlined his frame, making him seem a little surreal. He was a powerful-looking man, even in that suit. She supposed she should have counted herself lucky that he hadn't broken any of her bones when he tackled her in the yard.

"Don't you law enforcement types always want coffee?" she asked, trying her best to maintain a friendly atmosphere. Her mother always said that honey worked better than vinegar. "Or is that against some Secret Service agent code?"

Another dig. Still, after standing there for eight hours, he was hungry enough to eat a post. Coffee would help fill the hole in his stomach for the time being. "Coffee'll be fine" Nick heard himself saying.

With the fire illuminating the living room, he shut the door behind him. As he did so, he flipped the light switch.

Nothing happened.

Rising to her feet, Georgie paused, one hand fisted at her hip. Rather than be angry, she found herself mildly amused at this overdressed, albeit fine specimen of manhood.

"You want to play with the other switches, too?" she asked. She pointed to the kitchen and then down the hall. "There're about six more. None of them will turn on the lights either."

This was just getting weirder and weirder. "Why isn't there any electricity?"

"Because I don't have money to throw around," she suggested "helpfully." "There's no phone service either, so don't bother picking up the receiver." She nodded toward the phone on the kitchen wall. "If it makes you feel any better, they'll both be on in the morning. I got home ahead of schedule."

Ahead of schedule. That meant that he would have gone on waiting for her to arrive all night until the next morning.

The very thought of that intensified the ache in his shoulder muscles.

Of course, she could just be making the whole thing up and she and the pint-sized terror could have been coming back from visiting someone. "So you're sticking to your story about being out of town?"

"It's not a story, it's the truth," Emmie insisted angrily, stomping over to him, her hands on her hips, her head tilted back like a miniature Fury. "Mama doesn't lie. She says only bad people lie."

Georgie had her back to him. He watched the way her long braid moved as she arranged something in the hearth.

"No," he told the child while watching the mother, "sometimes good people lie, too."

Georgie straightened to go get the coffee pot from the cabinet in the kitchen. He was trying to trip her up, and he was just wasting his time. Because he had the wrong person. The sooner she convinced him of that, the sooner she could get down to the business of settling in.

"Ask anyone in town," Georgie urged him. The warm glow from the fireplace cast itself over her, coloring her cheeks, lightly glancing along her frame. "They'll all tell you the same thing. That I was out on the rodeo circuit. Around here, everybody knows everybody else's business." That used to annoy her. It didn't anymore. Now it just gave her a feeling of belonging.

"And what is it you do on the rodeo circuit?" Nick asked, not that he really believed her. Men who wore oversized hats and walked as if born on a horse hit the rodeo circuit, not a little bit of a woman with a big mouth and a child in tow.

"Win," Georgie answered tersely. "You'd better like your coffee black," she informed him, raising her voice as she walked into the small, functional kitchen and poured water into the battered coffee pot. "Because I don't have any milk handy. The last of it was used to drown a few chocolate chip cookies who were minding their own business about five hours ago."

Georgie looked at her daughter and grinned, remembering the snack they'd shared during the impromptu picnic she'd arranged for the little girl. She'd done it to lift Emmie's spirits because her daughter had been so sad about leaving the rodeo circuit. Georgie had talked at length about the ranch in glowing terms, reminding her daughter about all the people who loved her and were looking forward to celebrating her fifth birthday next week right here in Esperanza. By the time the cookies were gone, Emmie couldn't wait to get home.

"Black'll do fine," he told her.

As he watched, he saw Georgie stretch up on her toes, trying to reach the two white mugs on the top shelf. Crossing over to her, he took the mugs down and placed them on the counter. Georgie scooped them up and made her way back to the hearth.

He found himself following her.

Nick could feel Emmie's eyes boring into him, suspiciously watching his every move like some stunted hawk.

"This doesn't change anything," he warned Georgie,

referring to her effort at hospitality by making him something to drink.

"It's coffee, not a magic elixir," she responded. "I didn't think it was going to turn you into a prince. I'm just being neighborly."

"I'm not your neighbor."

"And for that, I am eternally grateful," Georgie told him. With the coffee brewing, she turned her attention to the center of her universe, her daughter. "Okay, Miss Emmie," she took Emmie's hand, "time to get you ready for bed."

But Emmie wiggled her hand out of her mother's grasp. Her large green eyes darted toward the stranger in their house, then back at her mother. "Mama, please?" Emmie pleaded.

In tune with her daughter, Georgie didn't need Emmie to spell it out for her. She could all but read her mind. Tired or not, there was no way the little girl was going to fall asleep a full three rooms away from here. Emmie was far too agitated about what was going on. She stood a better chance of having her daughter nodding off here, safely in her company.

Georgie surrendered without firing a shot. "Okay, pumpkin, take the sofa."

Relief highlighted the thousand-watt smile. Emmie wiggled onto the leather couch. "Thank you, Mama," she said happily.

Other than his own horrific childhood, Nick hadn't been around kids for more than a minute here or there. He had absolutely no experience when it came to dealing with them. Nor did he really want any. Kids had their own kind of logic and he had no time to unscramble that.

But his gut told him that what had just transpired was wrong from a discipline point of view. "You always let her win?" he asked Georgie.

Georgie watched him for a long moment, debating whether to tell him to butt out. But saying so wouldn't be setting a good example for her daughter. "I pick my battles," she told him. And, to be honest, she felt better being able to watch over Emmie right now. She didn't fully trust this character, Secret Service agent or not. "Arguing over everything never gets you anywhere."

"You could have fooled me."

"I have no desire to fool you, Mr. Secret Service agent—"

"My name's Nick Sheffield." He knew he was telling her needlessly. After all, she'd read as much on his ID—if she bothered reading it.

Georgie started again from the top. "I have no desire to fool you, Nick Sheffield," she told him. "I just want you to go away."

That made two of them, but under a different set of circumstances. "I'm afraid that's not going to happen right now," he informed her tersely.

Georgie sighed. "So much for *my* lucky streak continuing."

Behind her, the coffee pot had stopped percolating. She turned toward it, and, taking the two mugs she'd brought with her from the kitchen, she poured thick, black liquid into both. She set the pot back on its perch and brought the mugs over to him. Georgie offered him one.

He took it from her a bit leerily and she laughed. "Don't worry, I'm not going to pour it onto your lap." She couldn't resist a quick glance in that area. "Although the thought did cross my mind."

Thank God for small favors, he thought. But she'd stirred his curiosity. "Why not?"

"Because if I did that," she said only after she'd paused to swallow a mouthful, "then you'd think I was guilty. And I'm not," she pointed out.

"What if I think it anyway?"

"Then you're dumb," she told him simply. "Because that means that you're either not looking at the evidence—or ignoring it."

No, he thought, wrapping his hands around the mug, he had to admit that he wasn't looking at the evidence at the moment. He was looking at her. And God help him, he did like what he saw.

Chapter 4

Moving back toward the fireplace, Georgie pushed the coffee pot back on the grating. He heard her ask, "To your liking?" The woman didn't even bother looking over her shoulder as she carelessly tossed the words at him.

The question, coming out of the blue, caught him completely off guard. Was she referring to herself? Did she somehow sense that he was watching her, or was his reflection alerting her to the fact that he was studying her?

"What?"

"The coffee." Turning around, she nodded at the mug he was still holding in both hands. "Is it to your liking?"

Lost in his thoughts, some of which he shouldn't be having, Nick hadn't sampled the coffee yet. To rectify that, he took a sip—and discovered he had to practically chew the mouthful before he could swallow it. Accustomed to the coffee from a lucrative chain this offering she had prepared tasted almost raw to him. It certainly brought every nerve ending in his body to attention.

Nick cleared his throat after finally swallowing what he had in his mouth. He looked at her incredulously as she sipped, unfazed, from her mug.

"It's a little thick, don't you think?" he asked, pushing out each word. Was it coffee, or had she substituted tar?

Georgie seemed mildly surprised at his comment. "Most men I know like their coffee strong."

"You might not realize it, but there's a difference between strong coffee and asphalt."

Georgie lifted one shoulder in a careless shrug. "You don't have to drink it if you don't want to," she told him, reaching for the mug.

He drew the mug back out of her reach, knowing that to surrender it would somehow diminish him in her eyes. Nick had a feeling he was going to need all the edge he could get.

"That's okay," he assured the woman. "I'll drink it."

Nick saw a slight, amused smile curve the corners of her mouth. He had the uncomfortable feeling she was looking right through him. "Nobody said 'I double-dog-dare you,' Mr. Secret Service agent—sorry, 'Mr. Sheffield,'" she corrected herself. "If you don't like the coffee, don't drink it."

He held on to the mug anyway. "Just takes some getting used to." *Like you,* he added silently. Looking around at the darkened room, he changed the topic. "You really turned off the electricity."

A little slow on the uptake, aren't you, Sheffield? But she kept the observation to herself and replied, "That's what I said."

Then how had she sent those e-mails? he caught himself wondering. Eyeing her thoughtfully, Nick came up with the only alternative he could think of off the top of his head. "Then you took your computer with you?"

She thought of the refurbished tower and monitor she'd bought roughly six months ago, a couple of weeks before she'd gone back on the road with Emmie. She'd had the previous owner set it up for her, but personally had no interest in exploring its properties. It was like an alien entity to her.

She looked at him as if he'd lost his mind. "Now why would I do that?"

It took him a moment to realize she was serious. His own computer was almost an appendage with him. He took the notebook everywhere he went and couldn't conceive of a day going by without his checking his e-mail account. In his opinion, doing so was what kept the world small and manageable. He liked being in control, in the know. This was the best way.

"To stay in touch," he finally said when he saw that she was waiting for a response.

Georgie frowned. The man was obviously just another drone. Too bad, but then, what had she expected? He worked for the government. A clone without an imagination—except where it didn't count.

"They've got phones for that, Sheffield." She could see that her answer didn't make an impression on the Secret Service agent. "As I said before, I don't believe in computers," she told him. "I don't believe in sitting on my butt, sending messages to people I don't know—" what the hell was a "chat room" anyway? "—and living vicariously through someone else's stories. I'm out there, every day, experiencing life, I don't have to get mine secondhand." And then she gave him a reason she was certain he couldn't argue with. "Besides, my computer is too damn big to cart around across the state."

It was time he stopped trading words with this woman and start investigating. He was better at that anyway.

He'd already given the inside of the house a once-over when he'd first arrived on the property. "That tower in the bedroom room is the only computer you have?"

"Yeah. Why? How many computers do you have?"

Presently, he owned three. He had the one in his office at the Senator's headquarters, plus a full-sized one in his apartment. And, of course, there was the one that he always took with him, the notebook that contained everything the other two did, plus more. But he had no intention of telling her anything.

"This isn't about me," he reminded her.

Georgie lifted her chin defensively. Every time she started to think that maybe the man was human, he suddenly sprang back to square one all over again. It was like trying to take the stretch out of a rubber band and having it snap back at you.

"It's not about me, either," she retorted tersely. "Whoever you're looking for," Georgie informed him, "it isn't me."

What else could she say? He laughed dryly. "Mind if I don't take your word for that?"

"I'd like to say that I don't mind—or care—about anything you do, but because it affects me and mine—" she glanced over toward the sofa and Emmie, who, by virtue of her silence, she knew to be asleep "—I do. I mind very much."

"Afraid of what I'll find?" Nick asked. He was

already on his way to her bedroom. The fact that she had it set up in her bedroom rather than out in plain sight told him that she was probably trying to keep her little girl away from it and unaware of what she was doing. From what he'd observed she was a decent mother.

"No, I'm afraid that you'll plant something," she shot back, abandoning her mug as she hurried after him. "Hey, do you have a search warrant?" she challenged, suddenly remembering that on the TV dramas she'd occasionally watched, they always asked for a search warrant before allowing the police to turn their homes upside down. "Well, do you?"

"*Patriot* Act," Nick cited, reaching her bedroom. The existence of the act allowed for shortcuts and he mentally blessed it now. "I don't have to have one."

"That has something to do with finding suspected terrorists," Georgie remembered. The second the words were out of her mouth, her eyes widened in utter stunned surprise. She could only come to one conclusion. "So now you think I'm a terrorist?" This was becoming too ridiculous for words.

"Lots of definitions of a terrorist," he told her, pushing open her door. The small bedroom had only moonlight, pouring in through the parted curtains, to illuminate it. "Not all of them come with bombs strapped to their chests. The definition of a terrorist is someone who brings and utilizes terror against their victim."

This time, when he entered the room, Nick noticed something that had escaped his attention the last time he'd looked around the bedroom.

The computer tower and small monitor were set up on a rickety card table with a folding chair placed before it. The set-up stuck out like a sore thumb. What hadn't stuck out—at first glance—was the rectangular item stashed underneath the table. Pushed far back, it was attached to both the computer and the monitor.

"What's that?" he asked her.

"What's what?" she snapped. Was he talking about the computer? He would have had to have been blind to miss it. Just because she had a computer didn't mean she was guilty of sending threatening e-mails to his precious Senator Colton.

Damn it, Clay had told her to keep a gun in the house and she would have, if Emmie wasn't around. Not that she thought the little girl would play with it. Emmie knew better than that. But she knew her daughter. In a situation just like the one that had gone down in the front yard, if there'd been a gun around, Emmie would have grasped that instead of the tire iron—and used it. Emmie was very protective of her.

Almost as protective of her as she was of Emmie.

As she watched, Sheffield toed the rectangular object under the card table she'd put up. "This."

She looked down at it, then at him. Georgie shook her head. This was the first time she was seeing it. "I have no idea."

Squatting down, he used what moonlight was available to examine it. "Well, I do."

"Then why d'you ask?"

He ignored her annoyed question as he rose again to his feet. Nick dusted off his knees before answering. "It's a generator."

"No, it's not," she countered. She jerked her thumb toward the back of the house, beyond the bedroom. "The generator's outside, just behind this room—and it's broken," she added before Sheffield was off and running again. Repairing the generator was one of the things on her "see-to" list. The one that was almost as long as Emmie was tall. The house needed a lot of work, but because she was going to be home from now on and she was pretty handy, she figured she'd be able to finally get around to getting those things done.

If she could ever get rid of this man.

"Yes, it is," he informed her. "It's a portable generator."

As if to prove it, he switched the generator on. It made a churning noise, like someone clearing his throat first thing in the morning. The uneven symphony took a few minutes to fade.

Once all the lights on the machine's surface had come to life and ceased blinking, remaining on like so many small, yellow beacons, Nick rose and turned on the computer. It made even more noise than the generator, including a grinding noise that didn't sound too promising.

Georgie stared angrily at the portable generator. Sheffield had to have planted it earlier. There was no other way it could have gotten into her house. "That's not mine."

He ignored her protest. It was in her house, in her bedroom. Whose would it be if not hers?

The tower's hard drive continued grinding as it went through its paces. He half expected it to freeze up on him.

"You really should think about getting a laptop," he commented.

"What I should get," Georgie retorted, gritting her teeth, "is a gun so that I could keep trespassers off my property."

He wasn't listening. The grinding noise had finally abated and the hourglass had faded from the screen. Sitting gingerly down on the folding chair, he began to type. Braced for resistance, Nick found he was able to logon with no trouble. No password was necessary. The woman hadn't even taken the simplest of precautions. Go figure.

"And when you get that laptop," he commented, "you need to think about getting it encrypted."

Georgie watched him intently, convinced he would do something to her machine to make her look guilty. She only hoped she could stop him before he did it— not too likely because she had absolutely no idea what she was looking for him to do. "Encrypted?"

"Yes." He glanced at her for a second. She didn't know what he was talking about or she was pretending not to. "You know, password-access only. That way people wouldn't be able to get onto your computer."

She'd heard that if someone was really determined to get into your computer, they'd find a way. "But you would."

Nick couldn't help the tinge of satisfaction he felt from surfacing. He'd come a hell of a long way from that bully in the school yard.

"Yes," he agreed, "I would."

She crossed her arms before her, watching his fingers fly across the keyboard. Something was not right about a man being able to type that fast. Hands like that should be roping in a steer, not typing.

"So the people I should be protecting myself against with that password thing could still—what's the word? Hack?—into my computer."

"That's the word," he confirmed. "Hack." Nick laughed under his breath, although there was no humor to the sound. She played the innocent well, he'd give her that. "Guess you're right. Having a password wouldn't help. It would be pointless."

An uneasiness descended over her as she listened to

the keys clicking on the keyboard. "So is your nosing around on my computer," she insisted.

Bingo, he thought. He'd gotten into her online account and accessed her recent activities. It was right there in living color.

"Oh, I don't know about that." Rising from the chair, he started to turn the monitor toward her so that she could see what he knew she was already familiar with. He felt the card table begin to wobble.

Quickly bracing it, Nick muttered a few choice, ripe words under his breath. They mingled with his suppressed sigh.

Well, that hadn't taken very long, he thought sarcastically. And he had just begun entertaining the idea that maybe, just maybe, she was telling him the truth about not having sent those e-mails. Just went to show that con artists came in all sizes and shapes. Even pleasing ones.

Especially pleasing ones, he reminded himself. People like the Grady woman capitalized on their looks.

So much for believing in fairy tales, he thought. He raised his eyes to hers. Tapping the screen, he asked, "Do you know what this is?"

Georgie narrowed her eyes into angry green slits. "A frame-up."

Not by a long shot, he thought. "It's the Senator's Web site. And these," he pointed to communication at the bottom of the screen, "are the e-mails you sent to him just in the last couple of days."

Georgie forced herself to look at the screen. The e-mail Sheffield was pointing to was particularly venomous and it was signed "Lone Star Girl." But that was no proof that it was her.

This was surreal, she thought, fighting off a feeling

of desperation. This wasn't happening. She was asleep, that was it. She'd fallen asleep behind the wheel of the truck and maybe even crashed into a ditch. She was having hallucinations.

This *had* to be a hallucination.

This was real. He was real. And he was lying. She didn't know how he'd managed to do it while she was watching him, but somehow, he'd gotten that e-mail onto the computer.

Her jaw hardened. "No, I didn't." And there was no way he was going to get her to say that she did.

No more games, Nick thought. It was time to wrap this up. He pointed to the screen again. "Proof's right here. This is your computer, your account."

"I don't care if that damn message is painted across the Grand Canyon," she informed him hotly, tired of being intimidated. "I didn't write to your precious Senator. I don't even *have* an e-mail account."

"Then what's this?" he asked.

She threw up her hands. How the hell did she know how it got there? "A mistake. A glitch. I don't know. Machines are prone to errors." Her eyes blazed as she glared at him. "Nothing is foolproof and this proves it."

She'd emphasized the word "fool." Another dry laugh escaped his lips as he shook his head. "Calling me names isn't going to help you."

But strangling him might, she thought angrily. Georgie struggled to draw her patience to her and sound calm. "Look, I'm only going to say this one more time. I haven't been home in the last five months. The computer has. Somebody—"

Georgie clamped her mouth shut as her own words and the thought behind them resonated in her head. Sheffield hadn't planted this. Somebody had broken in. That had to be it. And if they broke in, there had to be evidence that they'd been here, right? Things would have been moved around, maybe the drawers had been ransacked. Something, anything, to show that someone had trespassed on her property, maybe even stolen her identity.

The idea took root, shaking her down to her very toes. Her throat tightened. Maybe she was overreacting. Oh, God, she hoped so.

Without another word, Georgie spun on the worn heel of her boot and hurried from the bedroom. The second she was out in the hall, she made a beeline for the kitchen.

Catching him off guard, it took Nick a second to realize that she'd bolted. He immediately hurried after her. Unable to refute him, she was making a break for it, he thought. Not on his watch. Not after he'd stood all those hours in this god-forsaken place, waiting for her.

"You can't run!" he called after her.

The woman didn't bother to answer him.

Expecting her to dart into the living room to grab her daughter, Nick was more than a little stunned to see Georgie run into the kitchen instead.

Was there a back door? Was she abandoning her daughter and making a run for it?

Nick strode into the kitchen after her and grabbed her by the wrist just as she'd reached the counter, spinning her around.

"Let me go!" she cried in outraged frustration. She struggled to yank her wrist out of his grasp.

For a little thing, she was pretty strong, he thought. Had to be all that rodeoing stuff she claimed to be doing.

Well, it wasn't going to do her any good. As a girl, she was strong, but she was no match for him.

"It'll go a lot easier on you if you surrender," he counseled.

"The hell it will."

Ever since she was a little girl, she'd hated the word "surrender." It meant weakness to her and she would rather die than admit to that.

Still trying to pull out of his grasp, Georgie raised her knee the way instinct and her older brother Clay had taught her, determined to award Sheffield the kind of pain that would make him set her free.

But Nick anticipated her move. "Oh, no, you don't," he cried.

Twisting, he jerked out of the way, throwing her off balance, then bodily pushed her against the wall. Pressed up against her, with his adrenaline running high and her breath hot against his chin, it took Nick a second to catch himself because his body was reacting to hers, taking him to places that his training did not allow for.

For two cents, he'd kiss that mouth of hers into silence.

It would have been the costliest two cents he would have ever had to pay and he knew it.

"You can't run," he told her, his breath coming in short spurts.

"I'm not running, I just want to get a damn flash-light," she cried.

Everything inside of her was scrambling madly—and anger had very little to do with it.

Chapter 5

Georgie's words burrowed through the wall of preconceived notions in his head. This matched none of them.

"A flashlight?" he asked.

Georgie glared up at him, doing her best not to think about the havoc his closeness caused within her. How could she be so angry and react to him on a far different level at the same time?

"Yes," Georgie hissed. "A flashlight."

Nick released her and took a step back—as much for her sake as his own. He wasn't the kind who usually entertained temptation, much less succumbed to it, but right now, he had to admit temptation was an irritating and unwanted guest.

"Why didn't you say so?" he fairly growled at Georgie.

She tossed her head, trying to ward off the effects of being so close to him. "I didn't realize I had to ask for permission to get something in my own house."

"We Secret Service agents are a jumpy lot," he told her drily. "Sudden moves make us nervous."

She looked at him for a long moment, unable to gauge whether he was serious. "I guess that means you don't attend many rodeos," she finally said.

"Never felt the urge." Although he found himself oddly curious about the events that would entice the likes of someone who looked like her to participate— if she was telling the truth and that was a big "if." He asked a question that was more to the point. "What do you need the flashlight for?"

Turning around, Georgie opened one of the drawers beneath the counter and took out the flashlight she kept there. She flipped it to the On position and it cast a waning beam.

The batteries were running down, she thought. Something else she needed to see to. The mental list was growing.

"So I can tell ghost stories." For a second, she put the flashlight beneath her chin so that it cast an eerie illumination on her face. And then she lowered it, as well as her sarcastic tone, again. "What do you think I need it for?"

He laughed drily. The woman was one for the books. "With you, my first guess probably wouldn't be the right one."

She had no patience with playing games, not with him, not now. She pointed the flashlight away from him. "I want to look around to see if anything's been taken or misplaced."

Again, she couldn't begin to imagine why anyone would want to break into her ranch house, other than for shelter during a storm. She had no hidden money stashed away in a wall safe, no valuable pieces of jewelry stuffed beneath her mattress or even any high-tech electronic equipment lying around. Everything she had—except for Emmie—she had either bought secondhand or had been given as a hand-me-down.

"Because you think someone broke in."

From his tone, she surmised that he still didn't believe her. "Yes, I think that someone broke in. That generator isn't mine."

"Someone broke in and brought you something rather than stealing something."

He was mocking her. She knew it sounded pretty stupid, but she didn't appreciate his pointing it out or using that tone with her. Her hand tightened around the neck of the flashlight. For a split second, she wished she was Emmie's age and had an excuse to act on her impulses. She would have loved to have hit this man and his mocking tone into the latter half of next week.

But she reined in herself and fell back on using logic and reason—even if he didn't have any. "You said you found the door unlocked."

"I did."

Well, that cinched it for her, if not for him.

"I always lock the door when I leave the house." She saw him look at her with doubt. She just *knew* he was going to say something again about people in rural areas being trusting. So she headed him off. "Times aren't what they used to be," she explained. "I trust my neighbors, but as you've just proven, people other than neighbors can come by. Those are the ones I lock my door against." And then she sighed, shaking her head as she began to scan the area with her flashlight. "Without much success, apparently," Georgie added under her breath, but audibly enough for Nick to overhear.

He was about to make a comment on what she'd just said when he saw her freeze. He saw nothing that would cause her to stop talking.

"What?"

She aimed her flashlight directly at what had caught her attention. She wasn't the world's best housekeeper, but she kept things neat, especially when she was going away.

"There's a newspaper by the window seat." Still aiming the flashlight on the paper, Georgie quickly crossed to the window seat.

Nick fell into step behind her. "So?"

She picked up the newspaper and, with the flashlight in one hand, looked at the date on the front page. "So, it's from last week." She dropped the newspaper back on the window seat.

He still didn't see what she was getting at. "Again, so?"

Did she have to hit him over the head with it? "I wasn't here last week."

That again. Nick shook his head, his skepticism all but shining like a beacon. "So you say."

She was tired of his not-so-veiled accusations. Tired of protesting and saying the same thing, over and over again.

"I can give you a list of the towns I've been in. I pretty much shadowed the circuit. I entered one if not more events in each town. People saw me. My daughter thinks I'm special, but even so, I haven't found a way to be in two places at the same time." And if that didn't make him shut up and finally go away, she didn't know what would.

The faintest hint of amusement lifted the corners of his mouth. "Would you want to be?"

What kind of a question was that? Was he deliberately trying to hassle her? Of course he was. Well, then, she just wouldn't let him, that's all.

Raising her chin, she gave him an answer she was fairly certain he couldn't argue with.

"Every mother wants to be in two places at once, if she's worth anything. She wants to be with her child and she wants to be doing whatever it is she needs to do to earn a living for that child." At least, that was the way she'd felt since the day Emmie was born and she'd fallen instantly and madly in love with the tiny baby. Taking her along with her on the rodeo circuit was the closest she could come to being with Emmie and still earn a living for them at the same time.

She had passion, he'd give her that. Passion that unfortunately drew him in. It took effort for him to mentally pull back. "Is that supposed to convince me that you're innocent?"

Maybe she *would* give in to her impulse and just smack him. It wasn't as if Sheffield didn't deserve it. "No, my innocence is supposed to convince you that I'm innocent."

Instead of commenting on her claim, Nick looked at her thoughtfully. She looked damn sincere. "How long do the events that you participate in last? Your portion of them," he elaborated.

She shrugged, thinking. "I don't know. Five, six minutes maybe." Although there were times, like when her horse had stumbled last year, when it had felt like an eternity—going by in slow motion. "Why?"

"Five, six minutes," he repeated. "So you wouldn't have to hang around all day if you didn't want to, would you? Just show up for your part of the contest and then you could leave."

She knew what he was getting at. Obviously he thought the events were all close by. Either that, or the man thought she had some kind of magical horse that flew her home and back. If she had a magical horse that could fly, she wouldn't have to be competing on the rodeo circuit in the first place.

But instead of telling him that, or what kind of an asinine blockhead she thought he was, she said something she knew he could understand. "I've got people to vouch for me."

She saw Sheffield raise a skeptical eyebrow. "Friends?"

"Yes, friends." Something she doubted that Sheffield had.

His expression didn't change. "Friends lie for friends."

There was no winning with this man. Or reasoning for that matter. Her frustration rose another notch. She struggled to keep her voice down in order not to wake Emmie.

"Are you determined to arrest me?"

He tried to sound impartial, even though right now, everything *did* point to her.

"I'm determined to make the threatening e-mails stop and have whoever has been sending them up on charges because, in case you didn't know, it's against the law to threaten a candidate for the presidency of the United States."

She resented his implication. That she was some hick who had no knowledge of the law. They weren't that far from San Antonio and even if she hadn't been to college, she'd been to the school of hard knocks and she'd graduated at the top of her class.

"Yes, I know that," she said between gritted teeth, "And again, *no* I didn't do it. Now someone, as you so cleverly pointed out by pulling up the Web thingy on my computer—"

"Web site," he supplied, interrupting her.

"Whatever," she said, struggling to rein in her temper. "Someone did and according to you, they did it from here. I know it wasn't me, so by process of elimination, it had to have been someone else. *Someone who broke in,*" she emphasized. "I don't know who or why, but it *wasn't* me. I don't know how else to say it." She'd pretty much reached the end of her rope here. *"IT WASN'T ME,"* she enunciated the words close to his ear so that not even a single syllable was lost on him.

"There's a newspaper I didn't bring in on the window seat and a dinky generator I never saw before stashed under my card table. Someone's been here." Her eyes blazed as she looked up at him. "Now you can believe me or not, I really don't care. But I do intend to get to the bottom of this because my house has just been violated and I don't like it."

Marching away from him, she returned to the kitchen and reached for the wall phone.

Nick snapped to attention and quickly cut the distance between them until he was right next to her. "Who are you going to call?"

It had been over four years since she'd found herself answering to anyone. She'd been more or less on her own since then and it grated on her nerves to be bombarded with questions like this—and expected to answer them.

"Somebody who knows I don't lie," she bit off. Lifting the receiver, she began pressing the buttons before she even had the phone to her ear. "The sheriff. Hey, what are you doing?" she cried. The agent's hand had covered hers and he pushed the receiver back down on the hook.

"I can't let you do that," Nick told her simply.

"Why?" she demanded. In the front yard, when she'd threatened to call the sheriff on him, he'd told her to go right ahead. Why was he changing his mind now? "You said I could."

"There's a little matter of jurisdiction."

"This is outside of Esperanza. That puts it into the sheriff's jurisdiction," she retorted. "He's the sheriff for the entire county."

"The e-mails are threats against a United States Senator," he reminded her. "That makes it a federal case."

Incredibly frustrated and stymied, Georgie wanted to scream. "I bet you like making a federal case out of everything."

Nick didn't rise to the bait she'd dangled in front of him and made no comment.

Desperate, not sure what the man was going to do next but fairly certain she wouldn't like it, Georgie tried to appeal to his better nature—if he had one.

"Look, Sheffield, I need someone who knows me. Someone who can make you believe that I'm not lying. Someone who can make you understand that I never sent any of those e-mails." *Because I sure can't.*

He supposed there was no harm in throwing her a bone. And there could be a very slim chance that she was telling the truth.

"Okay, let's just say for the sake of argument, you're right," he told her. "You're innocent. You're not the one sending those e-mails." Nick paused, the import of his own words replaying themselves in his head. If what she was suggesting was true, then that shifted the focus. This could be about her, not the Senator.

Or, that could be what she wanted him to think.

Nick explored the first question. "Why would

someone set this up to make it look as if you were threatening the Senator's life?"

How many times did she have to say it? "I don't know." She uttered each word carefully so that maybe this time, it sank in. "If I did, believe me I would tell you."

His mind whirling, he hardly heard her. "Do you have enemies?"

She shrugged. She didn't like to think so. "I don't know. Everyone's got enemies, I suppose. But nobody I know wants to see me in prison. Not even Kathy Jenkins."

Nick's interest was immediately aroused. They had a name. "Kathy Jenkins?" he repeated, his manner coaxing her to continue.

"I beat her in the barrel racing events in the last three towns."

The surge of adrenaline subsided as suddenly as it had begun. Nick sincerely doubted that all this was about barrel racing.

He tried again. "Nobody has it in for you? Your ex-husband? A jilted boyfriend? Some girl whose boyfriend you stole?" With each question, he watched her face for a reaction. Instead, he saw a wall going up.

"You always think the worst of people?" she asked.

"It's my job."

"If my daughter wasn't sleeping in the other room, I'd tell you what you could do with your job." Blowing out a breath, she went down the list he'd just raised. "There's no ex-husband," she deliberately avoided his gaze, wanting to see neither pity nor judgment in his eyes, "there's no jilted boyfriend and the only thing I ever 'stole' wasn't a boyfriend. It was a twenty-five cent candy bar when I was six. My mother made me give it back and apologize. I worked off my 'offense' by straightening bottom shelves in the grocery store for Mr. Harris for a month."

He could almost see that. She probably looked a lot like her daughter at that age. "Sounds like a strict mother," he commented.

Georgie instantly went on the defensive. "She was a good mother."

Well, there was a sore point, he thought. He wondered why.

"Didn't mean to imply otherwise," he told her. Nick looked at her for a long moment, common sense wrestling with a budding gut feeling—or was that just temptation in another guise? "I'll look into it," he finally said.

It had been so long between comments, she wasn't sure what he was talking about. "Excuse me?"

"Your alibi."

She hated the way that sounded, as if a lie was immediately implied. She didn't have an "alibi," she had a life. But in this case, she supposed having an alibi was a good thing.

"Then you believe me?"

He'd always played things very close to the vest. It was better that way—for everyone. "Let's just say I'm trying to keep an open mind."

He didn't strike her as someone who normally kept an open mind. "I guess maybe Emmie's hitting you with the tire iron did some good."

"Don't push it," he advised. "I just don't want to be wrong."

"I wouldn't want you to be wrong either," she told him pointedly. The subject of logistics occurred to her. "Does this mean you're going to be staying here?"

He nodded slowly. It wasn't something he was happy about, but this was going to take at least a day, if not more.

"For now."

"I've got a guest room in the back." She jerked her thumb toward the rear of the house.

He knew that. He'd done a very thorough surveillance of the house when he'd first gotten here, thinking he'd find the perpetrator at home.

The room in question was full of boxes filled with all kinds of things, none of them new. "You're using it for storage."

"There's a bed in there," she volunteered. The boxes were piled on top and all around it. "You're welcomed to it."

He could just see her trying to wall him in. "Here's just fine."

Here? Did he mean to stretch out on the sofa? She supposed she could move Emmie and hope the little girl went on sleeping. Unlike her brother Ryder, who could sleep while being tossed around in the funnel of a twister, Emmie was easily roused.

Moving over to the sofa, she began to pick up her daughter.

As with the flashlight, Nick caught her wrist and stopped her. "What are you doing?"

She wished he would stop touching her. "Moving Emmie so that you can have the sofa."

"Leave her where she is," he instructed, releasing her wrist. "I don't want the sofa. I'll take the chair." He nodded toward it.

Toward the left of the sofa, the item under discussion was an overstuffed chair that had once belonged to her grandfather, the famous rodeo star she'd been named after and whose last name she'd taken when she began riding herself. George "Rattlesnake" Grady. He'd favored that chair for some fifteen years and it still retained his shape. She loved it dearly, but it was hardly comfortable enough for Sheffield to spend the night in.

Georgie eyed him dubiously. "You won't get much sleep in it."

"I don't intend to sleep."

Which meant that he intended to watch her, she thought, immediately suspicious. And that in turn put them back in two separate camps.

Still, he wasn't slapping handcuffs on her and shouting that she was under arrest. She supposed that she could deal with anything short of that.

And come the morning, she promised herself, after she deposited her winnings into the bank, she'd find a way to set Mr. Secret Service agent straight.

Once that happened, her life as Georgie Grady, rancher, could finally begin.

Chapter 6

"What?"

Georgie stared across the counter at the bank teller as if he were babbling gibberish.

It was just a little after nine in the morning and Georgie stood in the center window of the First Western Bank. Of the two banks housed in Esperanza, First Western was the older, more established one. That was why she'd originally chosen it. Safety and stability had always been exceedingly important to her.

Getting here this morning was a semi-victory on her part. A victory because that Secret Service agent who'd invaded her life hadn't wanted her to go into town. Semi because in order to leave the house at all, she'd had to accept that he was accompanying her. He'd told her in no uncertain terms that he wouldn't allow her to leave his line of sight for more than five minutes. Five minutes being the amount of time, according to the insufferable man, that a person should be able to take a shower and get dressed again. She hadn't bothered pointing out how ridiculous that was because she'd been in a hurry to get to the bank to put her money away.

Because she'd been in a hurry, Georgie had given in to him and even agreed to let him drive Emmie and her in his sedan. All she'd wanted to do was to get to the bank to make this final deposit.

And now all she wanted was not to throw up. Within the last minute, her stomach had twisted into a knot and then risen up into her throat.

If only she could do the last few minutes over again. Walk in, nod at the teller and have the man take her deposit slip with a smile, and not say what he'd just said.

She just couldn't have heard him correctly.

Javier Valdez looked at her over the tops of his small, rimless glasses. "I said I guess we're going to have to open an account for you."

That made absolutely no sense.

A feeling of impending doom tightened about her throat. She fought to ignore it.

"But I already have an account," Georgie reminded him. To back her up, she pushed forward the bankbook she'd brought with her, along with her deposit slip and the money she'd won during the last five months. "This one. Trudy Miles opened it for me the day before she retired," she remembered. "It was the same month that Emmie was born."

The month she'd realized that she wasn't a child anymore. Eighteen or not, she was a mother. A mother with responsibilities. Clay had given her the hundred dollars that she'd deposited that day. It was a gift for

Emmie, her brother had told her. He was giving her money because he "wasn't any good at buying stuff for babies." Georgie could remember tearing up as she'd made that first deposit.

Now tears threatened to come for a completely different reason.

Javier frowned. "But you closed that account," he told her gently. "Said you lost the bankbook so we had to match up your signature. Don't you remember?"

That was impossible. She hadn't been here in five months. She *hadn't*.

"You saw me?" she challenged. Behind her, she heard Sheffield shifting his weight. Probably getting ready to handcuff her and lead her off, she thought. With all her heart, she wished the man was somewhere else. Preferably in hell.

"Everybody saw you," Javier told her with a soft laugh. "That red hair of yours is hard to miss." He smiled at her. A widower, it was obvious that he was a little smitten with her. "Nobody else around here's got hair the color of a Texas sunset."

"But that's not possible," Georgie insisted.

Listening to the exchange between the Grady woman and the bank teller, Nick found himself thinking that the distress and anguish in her voice sounded genuine. She was probably an accomplished actress. Most con artists were and this was beginning to take on the shape of a con.

But still, he couldn't quite shake off the effect of her voice.

Moving forward so that he stood beside Georgie, Nick appraised the short, dark-haired teller. "Were you the one who closed the account for her?"

Javier's black eyes darted toward Georgie, as if to

silently ask if it was all right for him to answer the question. "Is he with you?"

Beads of sweat slid down her spine at the same time a chill took hold of her. Javier's voice echoed in her head. It took her a second to make sense of the question. She was doing her best to block the onslaught of some very terrifying thoughts.

"For now, unfortunately, yes," she reluctantly acknowledged.

Javier's eyes shifted back to the tall man beside Georgie. "No, I didn't. Mr. Welsh did."

"Can you get him over here?" Under no circumstances could that be mistaken for a request. It was a tersely worded command.

One that clearly made Javier nervous. Sheffield probably got a lot of that, Georgie thought. And he probably reveled in it. Right now, she didn't care what the Secret Service agent did as long as he got this mess untangled for her.

Clearing his throat, Javier shook his head. "No, I can't."

Georgie felt Sheffield take a half step closer. The very movement seemed intimidating to Javier. She saw the man's eyes widen.

"And why's that," Nick's eyes dipped down to the teller's name tag. "Javier?"

"Mr. Welsh is on vacation," Javier recited, never taking his eyes off the man beside Georgie. "His daughter's getting married in Colorado, so he and Mrs. Welsh went there."

Pretty convenient, Nick thought. "When did he leave?"

Javier looked like a man whose mind had gone blank. And then, mercifully, he recovered. Partially. "A few days ago."

"Can you get him on the phone?" Nick asked in the same no-nonsense monotone.

Was he actually going to help her? Georgie wondered. The thought made her feel a little better.

Javier opened and closed his mouth several times without actually saying anything intelligible. A squeak emerged. Flustered, he glanced over his shoulder at the small row of desks lined up against the wall.

"Mr. Collins?" Javier's voice cracked as he squeezed out the bank manager's name. "Could you come here, please?"·

A tall, somewhat heavyset man in his thirties came over after pausing to close a folder on his desk. Crossing to the teller's window, Allen Collins offered Georgie a genial smile.

"Nice to see you again so soon, Georgie. Emmie," he nodded at the child. "Change your mind about closing your account?"

This was some awful nightmare. It had to be. "I didn't close my account. I haven't been here," she insisted. "I've been on the road. Winning this." She pushed the neatly banded pile of checks forward. "There's got to be some mistake." She silently pleaded with him to agree.

Nick's eyes shifted from the bank manager's face to Georgie's profile. The teller's statement dovetailed nicely to back up the fact that the Grady woman had been here all along, churning out poisonous e-mail. That was his intellectual take on the situation. His gut, however, said something else. Her eyes conveyed that her whole life had been turned upside down. It had him doubting the validity of his own theory.

"No, no mistake," Collins assured her. In the face of

her insistence, his expression seemed just a shade uneasy. Suddenly, he held up his right index finger, indicating that she needed to wait for a moment. The manager crossed back to his desk and the old-fashioned rectangular metal file box he kept there. Flipping through it, he found what he was looking for. Collins removed a single index card and brought it back with him to the window.

Placing the card on the counter, he turned it around so that she could see. "See, there's your signature, plain as day."

Georgie stared numbly at the card. The signature was dated last week. It matched the original one from five years ago down to the circle over the letter *i*.

Was she losing her mind? Or was someone playing a horrible joke on her?

All she could do was repeat what she knew to be true. "I didn't sign this."

"But that's your signature." At this point, the smile on the bank manager's face wore thin.

Georgie was afraid to look at Sheffield, afraid of what she'd see on his face. Smug triumph. What the bank manager was saying made it look as if she'd lied to Sheffield about her whereabouts. As if she'd been here all the time, conducting her life. Raiding her bank account and sending threatening e-mails to damn Joe Colton.

But it wasn't true. None of it.

Stubbornly, Georgie shook her head. "Someone must have forged it. I didn't sign the card, I didn't close the account." Her voice rose as she enunciated each word. "I *wasn't* here."

"Mama was with me, riding in the rodeo," Emmie piped up. The pint-sized defender added in a logical voice, "Somebody stole our money." And then she turned around to look at the man who'd come with them. "Are you going to help us get our money back?"

No way was this a four-year-old, Nick thought. She had to be one of those midgets—what was it they called themselves these days? Little people? She was one of them. And right now, this little person was putting him on the spot.

Rather than answer her directly—he had no idea how to have a conversation with someone too young to vote—Nick looked at the bank manager.

"You have surveillance cameras in this place?" he asked Collins.

The bank manager took offense. The smile on his face vanished without a telltale trace. "Just because we're a little off the beaten path doesn't mean that we're primitive."

Nick heard what he needed to hear. "I take that as a yes. Mind if I see the footage from the day Ms. Grady was supposed to have closed her account?"

Collins squared his shoulders. "I'm afraid that's highly irreg—"

Nick stopped him by taking out his badge and ID and holding them up in front of the man.

The man's small, brown eyes darted back and forth, reading the information over twice, before he finally raised them to look at his face. "Secret Service?" he asked uncomfortably.

Nick's own expression was impassive, giving nothing away. "Yes."

Collins and Javier both gazed uncertainly at Georgie. Collins found his tongue first. "This is a government matter?"

"It's complicated" was all Nick would say.

"No, it's not," Georgie cried, turning toward him. Her bank account had nothing to do with the government. "Someone's stolen my money." She thought of the e-mails, the ones she hadn't sent. Was there a connection? Had someone done all this to get back at her for something? Or was this a random attack? "And my identity."

"Georgie, you don't look so good," Javier observed. There was concern on his drawn face. "You want a glass of water or to sit down, maybe?"

"What I want," she replied, desperately trying to get a grip, "is my money."

This couldn't be happening. By her reckoning, with this last batch of winnings, she should have been up to a little more than three hundred thousand dollars. More than enough to buy her some time and some peace of mind before she decided what she wanted to do with the rest of her life. Instead, someone had wiped her out. All she had left were the winnings in her hand. Thank God for that.

And then, as if she wasn't already reeling from this unexpected turn of events as well as being accused of terrorism by computer, something else suddenly occurred to Georgie.

Oh, dear God, no.

Georgie struggled to keep her hands from shaking as she pulled her wallet out of her back pocket. Flipping it opened, she took out her credit cards. There were four in all. She clutched them for a moment, as if that could somehow keep them safe. Keep them hers.

Watching her, Nick frowned. Now what? "What are you doing?"

Georgie's breath grew shallow. She wasn't going to panic, she wasn't. She knew if she did, she'd scare

Emmie. As it was, she was scaring herself. But this thing was just mushrooming. Before answering, she turned the cards face down one by one.

Picking up the first one, she searched for a toll-free number. "I've got to make some phone calls," she told him, hoping against hope that she was wrong. The sickening, metallic taste in her mouth told her she probably wasn't.

The expression on the manager's face turned compassionate. "You're welcome to use the phone on my desk, Georgie."

She nodded, murmuring, "Thank you."

The manager beckoned her over to the far side of the bank, unlocking a swinging half door so that she and Emmie could enter.

Georgie felt as if she was moving in slow motion, trapped in a nightmare she couldn't wake up from. And all the while she kept telling herself that this couldn't be happening. She had been knocked down so many times before and had always managed to get up again. If the worst came to pass, she could do it again. But this time it would be harder. This time her daughter was old enough to understand what was happening.

Nick followed her, putting his hand out to stop the door as the manager began to close it after Georgie and her daughter had passed through.

"The tapes?" he prodded.

Embarrassed, the manager's face turned a light shade of red. "Yes, of course. Right this way." He led them to a small back room where all their monitors and tapes were kept.

Georgie was barely aware of Sheffield leaving. Very slowly, as if she'd just aged fifty years, she gripped the side arms and lowered herself into the manager's chair.

Taking a deep breath, she pulled the streamlined, black phone closer to her on the desk.

"It's gonna be all right, Mama," Emmie assured her quietly. She offered her mother a big, broad smile.

Georgie almost cried.

She looked into the small, perfect face. That was supposed to be her line. She was the one who was supposed to do the comforting, not be the one on the receiving end.

Doing her best to rally, she gave the little girl's hand a quick squeeze. "Of course it is, Emmie. I just have to make a few calls, get a few things straightened out, that's all."

Georgie hoped to God she sounded convincing.

"It was her." The manager repeated nervously as he entered the small, darkened room. Nick was directly behind him. "The tape'll prove it."

So he'd already said. But the more the manager echoed his statement, the less inclined Nick was to believe that Georgie had actually closed her account. Why go through this big act if she knew it was closed? For whose benefit?

The pieces just didn't fit together.

"Let's just see it" was all that Nick said in response.

He noted that the bank manager seemed to be growing more agitated. Because he'd made a mistake? Or because he was guilty of something? There was no way to tell—yet. This situation was getting messier by the minute.

"Right," Collins agreed, as if forcing himself to sound cheerful. Opening the deep drawer where surveillance tapes from the last month were kept, he rummaged around. "Somebody took them out of order," he complained. He read the dates marked on the side of the tapes under his breath. "Finally." He flashed a smile at Nick, then let it fade when all he got in response was a stony stare.

Plucking out of the drawer the tape in question, he held it up like a trophy. "Here it is," he declared with relief, as if the mere finding of the tape would somehow vindicate him.

Nick nodded toward the video player. "Play it," he instructed.

"Yes, of course." But Collins continued holding the tape in his hands in a manner that indicated he didn't know which end played. "Abby?" Collins turned toward the teller directly outside the small room where the video equipment was kept. "Would you play this for Mr. Sheffield?"

Abby entered dressed in a turquoise skirt so tight it resembled a tourniquet. Her eyes swept over Nick slowly, taking in every inch from head to toe. The appreciative smile was quick in coming.

She'd taken measure of him, Nick thought. As an expert on body language, he could tell she liked what she'd seen.

Abby took the tape from the manager, but her eyes remained on Nick. "It'll be my extreme pleasure," she purred.

Tape in hand, Abby sat down at the video recorder, taking care to sit slow enough to better show off the more compelling parts of her anatomy. Tucking her legs over to one side, she leaned forward and popped the tape into the machine. After glancing over her shoulder at Nick, she hit Play.

"Here we go," she announced.

The time stamp in the corner said it was nine o'clock, which was when the bank opened its doors. Nick had no desire to stand behind the brassy blonde and watch an entire day's worth of transactions.

"Fast forward it," he told her.

Again, she looked over her shoulder at him, her smile particularly seductive.

"Whatever you want," Abby said, her tone indicating that she was open to more than working the buttons on the machine.

Nick ignored her the way he did anything he didn't particularly care for. Focusing solely on the activity on the screen, he watched and waited. Customer after customer came and went across it, all of them resembling characters going through their paces in a keystone cops silent movie.

And then he saw her. Georgie. Tight jeans, work shirt, worn boots and all.

"Slow it down right there," he ordered. Abby complied. It was obvious she had no idea what he was looking for, nor did she want to know.

Nick caught his breath.

There, on the screen, with her telltale red braid hanging down to the small of her back, was Georgie Grady.

Chapter 7

"That's her," Collins said eagerly, needlessly pointing to the screen at the only bank customer on the monitor. There was relief in his voice as he added, "I told you she was here."

Nick ignored the man. He was too busy watching the woman, who was a dead ringer for Georgie, move up to the teller's window and place a briefcase on the counter between them.

"Keep going," he told Abby when she glanced up at him.

The teller on the tape disappeared for a moment. When he returned, he had an index card with him. The signature card, Nick assumed. Within moments of signing the card, the transaction was completed. The woman on the screen took back her briefcase, now filled with what he assumed were the proceeds from her account, and then hurriedly moved away. Nick watched the scene intently.

"Rewind," he instructed. When Abby did as he asked, he had her stop at the same place as before and watched the scene again. And then a third time.

Puzzled, Collins looked at him. "What is it you're looking for?"

Nick blew out a breath, still looking at the screen. "An explanation."

This time it was the teller who glanced up at him and asked a question. "For?"

"For starters, why 'Georgie' kept her head turned away from the camera the whole time." Was it just a coincidence, or was there a reason the woman on the screen had done that?

Something wasn't quite right and he couldn't put his finger on it. Yet. He told Abby to play the tape one more time.

"Most people don't even realize that there's a camera there," Collins told him, trying to be helpful. "Ms. Grady was probably lost in thought and just in a hurry to do whatever it was she wanted to do with all that money she withdrew."

"I know what I'd do," Abby commented. The smile on her lips was seductive as she gazed up at the tall, dark Secret Service Agent at her side.

"Uh-huh," Nick answered, lost in thought. It wasn't clear who the response was directed toward. "Play it again," he instructed.

Maybe he was making too much of this, Nick thought, watching the scene for the fifth time. Maybe he was looking for a zebra when there was a bucking horse right in front of him. After all, the bank manager was certain that the woman on the video tape was Georgie Grady and that did, after all, support his initial theory that the woman had been here all along, sending those threatening e-mails to the Senator that she'd denied having anything to do with it.

Here it was, all neatly gift wrapped for him with a bow on top and he was pushing it away, Nick upbraided himself.

All that was left to do was to arrest the woman and bring her back with him for prosecution.

So why was he hesitating?

Because his gut told him something wasn't right? Or because something a bit lower than his gut was muddying up his thinking?

No, damn it, he wasn't the type to let his personal feelings—when he even had them—to get in the way of his judgment. There *was* something wrong with what he was watching on the tape and he thought he finally had a bead on what it was.

A noise directly behind him had Nick quickly turning around, one hand on the hilt of the weapon he wore.

Georgie was in the doorway, her face ashen. Not because of the firearm. The woman had probably grown up around guns all of her life. No, there was a different reason for the lack of color in her face. One hand on the doorjamb, she looked as if she was struggling to stand up.

"You're on the surveillance tape," he told her, watching her reaction.

She didn't seem to hear him. Or, if she heard, the words apparently didn't penetrate. She made no response to his statement one way or the other.

"There are charges on my credit cards," she told him. The words sounded as if she was being strangled.

"That's what they're for, to charge things with," he replied.

Some of the color returned to her cheeks. She continued to hold on to the doorjamb for support.

"Charges I didn't make," she snapped.

It was official. The unthinkable had happened. Something she had never dreamed of *ever* happening, not to her. She'd read about this in the newspaper. But now she was the victim.

Her identity had been stolen.

Her identity, her money and her life.

Both of their lives, she amended, looking down at her little girl.

"Somebody's stolen my identity." Every single card she owned had been taken and used, even the two she kept as emergency backups, the two she *never* used except for once a year just to keep them active.

The simple sentence got her all of Nick's attention. "Are you sure?"

Georgie felt a wave of hysteria rising. Last night, she'd been flush, sitting on top of three hundred thousand dollars. This morning she was all but broke and fiercely in debt. And about to be arrested. How could everything have gone so wrong so fast?

"Of course I'm sure," she retorted angrily. Did he think this was a game? Why would she do that? What would she gain by pretending that her identity had been stolen?

Georgie unfolded the piece of paper she'd used while speaking to the customer service representatives at the four different credit card companies.

"There's a whole list of charges from stores on the damned Internet. Stiletto heels, fancy clothes, fancier undergarments." She pointed to the name of an exclusive shop that had only recently launched online sales. "CDs by people I wouldn't listen to, DVDs of movies I wouldn't be caught dead watching—"

The mention of stiletto heels and Maid of Paradise bras and microscopic panties had Nick's mind booking passage on a ship he couldn't allow to leave the harbor. Still, for one unguarded moment, he couldn't help imagining what she would have looked like, wearing only those items.

"Planning on doing some entertaining?" he quipped.

Her eyes blazed at the question and even more when she thought of the unknown person who had done all this to her.

"Planning on a murder if I ever get my hands on the person who's responsible for all this," she retorted.

He looked at her for a long moment, playing the devil's advocate. "You still say it's not you."

Georgie squared her shoulders, as if that could somehow help her get the point across more forcefully. "With my dying breath," she told him fiercely. "Not that you believe me." The last sentence fairly sizzled with her anger.

That was just the problem, Nick thought. He was starting to believe her.

He glanced at the bank manager who still stood at the desk. The man was obviously taking in every word and trying—without success—to look as if he wasn't.

"Make me a copy of that section of the tape," Nick instructed.

Clearly feeling that he was off the hook, Collins snapped to attention, more than happy to comply. "Right away," he promised.

Nick heard the bank manager murmuring to Abby,

telling her to make the copy because she was the one running the tape.

That taken care of, Nick took hold of Georgie's elbow and led her out of the small, dark room. Emmie hurried to follow.

"Let's just say," he told Georgie evenly, "for now, that I'm not a hundred percent convinced that that's you on the surveillance tape."

"Of course, it's not me. That's what I've been trying to tell you all along." She shrugged out of his hold. Wanting to remain aloof, curiosity got the better of her. "What makes you think it isn't me?"

"You walk differently." That was what had bothered him while he was initially watching the tape.

Georgie stared at him. She wasn't aware of there being anything unique about her gait. "What?"

Nick elaborated. "The woman on the tape was in a hurry, but she still walked like she knew everyone was watching her. She minced and put a little wiggle in her step. You walk like you've got somewhere else to be and you cut through that distance like a ranch hand. There's nothing feminine about the way you move." Other than her body, he added silently. But that was neither here nor there and certainly not something he was about to admit to her.

She wasn't sure if she was clear about what was going on here. "Are you insulting me or finally coming to my rescue?"

He didn't view it as either and he didn't care for the tone she was using. "I'm making an observation. You want my help or not?"

In a perfect world, Georgie thought, she would have lifted her chin, told him what he could do with his help.

She could handle the situation by herself. But this wasn't a perfect world and without doing a single thing to bring about this awful chain of events, she knew she was in way over her head. Like it or not, she had no recourse but to accept his offer.

Still, the words had a bitter taste in her mouth and burned her tongue as she said them. "I want it."

Nick felt something suddenly clutch his leg. Startled, he looked down to see that the woman's daughter had all but wrapped herself around him.

Emmie smiled up at him gleefully. "I *knew* you weren't as bad as you looked."

He kept forgetting that she was there, a pint-sized recorder with ears, taking in everything and absorbing it rather than letting it go over her head like the average four-year-old.

"You sure she's only four?" he asked Georgie.

"I'm almost five," Emmie announced proudly as her mother gently removed her from the Secret Service agent's leg and then protectively kept her hand on her shoulder. "Mama said we had to come back because Uncle Clay wants to help celebrate my birthday."

"Uncle Clay," Nick repeated, raising his eyes from the child to look at Georgie. "Is that what you have her call your boyfriends?" he asked mildly, giving no indication that her answer, one way or the other, meant anything to him. " 'Uncle?' "

"No, that's what I have her call my older brother." Overwrought, and stressed near to the breaking point, not to mention that she hadn't had any sleep because she'd spent the night verbally sparring with Sheffield, she glared at him. "Don't you pay attention? I said I didn't have a boyfriend."

As he looked at her, Nick found it hard to believe she was single. She was far more than passably pretty. Then again Georgie Grady could also slice any man to bloody ribbons with that sharp tongue of hers and he was fairly certain, given half a chance, that she would run over anyone who got in her way.

"Got that tape for you," Collins called out, coming up behind Nick. He held the tape aloft as if it was the pot of gold at the end of the rainbow.

Georgie shifted uncomfortably. Sheffield had said that he thought the woman in the tape was an impostor, disguised to make people think it was her. What if he was only putting her on? What if he was just saying that to make her put down her guard?

"What are you going to do with that?" she asked Sheffield. "Use it at my trial?"

He'd never believed in putting all his cards on the table until the game was over. This was far from over. "Maybe, maybe not. Right now, I'm going to have it expressed back to Prosperino in California and have my tech support see if he can clean up the picture and magnify the image."

The image. She noted that he didn't refer to the person in question as her. Georgie supposed that it was a start. "Okay."

He was going to need a padded envelope and postage. "This place have a post office?" He tossed out the question to both Collins and Georgie.

"A post office, two banks, a city hall and a sheriff's department. Some people even think we're close to civilized," Georgie answered with a trace of resentment at the way he'd dismissed Esperanza. It was all right for her to feel hemmed in by the town once in a while because she lived here and for the most part, she loved it. But he had no right to look down his nose at it. Or her.

About to comment on her quip, he decided to keep it to himself. He hadn't actually meant what he'd said as an insult, just that Esperanza felt so damn rural to him. He was accustomed to places like Los Angeles and New York where you could find whatever it was you needed within a very small radius.

"Show me" was all he said.

"Fine, I will." Still numb and shaken, Georgie turned on her heel to lead the way out of the bank.

"*We* will, Mama. I know where the post office is, too," Emmie reminded her.

The one bright spot in her life, Georgie thought, taking Emmie's hand in hers. "Sorry," she apologized. "*We* will," she said, correcting herself. Emmie's smile was positively beatific.

"Can we do anything else for you?" Collins called out after Nick.

"I'll let you know," Nick tossed over his shoulder without slowing his pace.

"Who are you calling?" he asked Georgie some twenty-five minutes later.

They'd gone to the post office and he'd gotten the tape off, sending it by overnight express. Once it was on its way, he'd called his tech to alert him to its arrival. Georgie had been unusually quiet through it all and he'd begun to think that maybe the events of the last day had her in a state of shock.

But now, sitting in the passenger seat in the dark sedan he'd rented, Georgie pressed a single button on her cell phone before placing it against her ear. Instead of answering him, she held up her finger, indicating that he'd have to wait his turn. It didn't exactly make him very happy.

"Hi, it's me," she said as someone on the other end apparently picked up. Nick listened, trying to put things together from only half a conversation. "Last night. Look, can you come on up to the house? Something's happened. No, not to Emmie, she's fine." He saw her turn and look over her shoulder at the little girl in the car seat as if to reassure herself. "No, I'm not hurt. Why do you always have to think the worst? Okay, okay, maybe I was a trifle melodramatic, but I really do need to see you." She paused to listen to the person on the other end, then said, "Good. 'Bye." She closed her phone again and slipped it into her front pocket.

"Who were you talking to?" Nick asked again.

Had she called for reinforcements? Was he making a mistake after all, giving her the benefit of the doubt about this? At the very least, he didn't relish the fact that someone else would be nosing around at her house while he was there.

"My brother. One of my brothers," Georgie amended.

These days, she tended to forget about Ryder. She didn't like to dwell on her other brother because then she'd have to think about how Ryder was faring in prison and she didn't like doing that. It made her worry about him despite the fact that he'd been found guilty by a jury of his peers and he had committed the offense that had landed him there. She couldn't help it. He was still, after all, her brother and she could remember him in better days. Remember him with a great deal of affection. Ryder wasn't bad, just misguided. Like her, he missed their mother. And, unlike her, he'd resented their older brother when Clay had taken over as the head of the family.

Nick spared her a look. "You've got more than one?"

He was going to make another call to Steve when he got the chance. He wanted to find out as much as he could about this woman.

"Two," she told him. "Clay and Ryder. Both older." And they both had the tendency to treat her like a child. At times, Clay still did, but then, he was the oldest and saw himself as more of a patriarch than a brother. "I was talking to Clay."

"Where's Ryder?"

She shrugged, deliberately looking out the window. "He's not around right now."

Nick picked up on the odd note in her voice. "Where is he?"

"Not here" was all she said.

It was bad enough that the people in town knew that her brother was in prison. She didn't want Sheffield knowing it as well. He'd probably think of them as being white trash or something equally demeaning. For that matter, she didn't want him to know anything about her family. Someone like Sheffield, with his black suit and his dark aviator sunglasses, would look down on the fact that her mother, a former rodeo star herself, had had an affair with a married man. And that he was a Colton.

In an act of self-defense, she leaned forward and turned up the radio a shade. He'd fiddled with the dials on the way over until he'd located an oldies station. She had nothing against old rock and roll songs, but when she was tense—and she was now and would remain so until everything was squared away again—nothing calmed her down like the familiar. In this case, that meant country and western songs.

She switched the dial over to one of several country and western stations broadcasted in the area. Out of the corner of her eye, she saw Sheffield's shoulders stiffen. Georgie smiled to herself.

Deal with it, she ordered him silently.

Because the woman apparently didn't seem to want to talk about her other brother, he let the subject drop. If he needed to know the whereabouts of this Ryder, he would. For now, he blocked out the tale of a broken-hearted cowboy, singing his tale of woe to the only dependable force in his life, his horse.

Nick sighed. Damn but he hated country music.

A tall, dark-haired, rangy-looking man sat on the front steps of the ranch house. The moment they pulled up in the yard, the man stood up, dusting off his jeans. Nick judged him to be in his mid-twenties. The set-in tan testified to his earning a living by working outdoors.

There was something self-assured about the cowboy. This was a man who led, not followed. Nick was on his guard instantly.

"Uncle Clay," Emmie cried, squirming out of the car seat and leaping from the car. She sailed gleefully into the man's arms as the latter squatted down, arms spread, just as she reached him.

"Man but I've missed you. You must've grown a foot since I last saw you. How's my favorite girl?" he asked, rising and swinging her around.

"I'm fine," Emmie declared. "But Mama's got troubles," she added solemnly.

Holding his niece to him, Clay turned to look at the

stranger with his sister as they both got out of Nick's sedan.

The man wasn't her type, Clay judged. Georgie didn't like men in suits and sunglasses. Too soft. As for him, he didn't trust a man whose eyes he couldn't see when he was talking to him.

"Is that the trouble right there?" he asked Emmie, nodded his head toward the stranger.

Emmie twisted around to see who her uncle was referring to. She giggled and shook her head. It was obvious to Georgie, who came to reclaim her, that her daughter had changed her mind about the man. "No, that's Nick."

Clay looked at the stranger grimly, his deep espresso-colored eyes growing hard. "What's a Nick?" he asked.

Chapter 8

For the space of one moment, Georgie struggled with the very strong desire to just fling herself into Clay's arms and tell him what had happened, starting with Sheffield tackling her in the front yard. Clay would take care of everything for her, the way he used to. The way he had when their mother died.

But she wasn't that little girl anymore. Even back then, she'd had a tendency to resist Clay's protective ways because to be taken care of carried a price tag. It meant surrendering her independence, and independence meant everything in the world to her. Hers had been hard won and it was a trophy she would fight to retain to her dying breath.

So rather than throw herself into her brother's arms, she stood where she was, holding herself in check as she smiled and greeted him warmly.

"Hi, Clay."

"Hi, yourself." Clay nodded at her. His sister had never been the easiest woman to deal with. She only accepted help under loud protest. That was why he'd been surprised when she'd called, saying she needed to see him. This was more like her. "Nice to see you back, rodeo queen. You home for good now?"

Nick noted that Georgie seemed to bristle at the nickname. Or maybe it was the question and the unspoken implication behind it—that her brother didn't want her out there, competing—that had her stiffening.

The laugh that passed her lips was short and rueful. "I was going to be."

Clay's dark eyes slanted toward the man with his sister before he asked, "But?"

Georgie blew out a breath. She was still struggling to get a grip, to stop feeling as if she'd been physically and emotionally violated. "There've been some nasty developments."

Clay's frown deepened. Again he looked at the man who'd gotten out of the driver's side of a dark four-door sedan. His brother radar had gone up the second he saw that. "Like?" he asked.

She did her best to sound removed from what she was saying. The words came tumbling out with no preface, no preamble. "Somebody stole all my money, Clay. And broke into my place while I was gone. Whoever did was sending threatening e-mails to Joe Colton—on my computer."

At the mention of the Senator's name, Clay murmured an ambiguous sounding "Oh."

There was a world of meaning hidden behind the

single word, Nick thought. Something was going on here that he wasn't getting—and he didn't like it.

Never one to mince words, Clay figured he'd held his peace long enough. He nodded toward the stranger. "What's he got to do with it?"

"I work for the Senator," Nick told him before Georgie could say anything. "And I came to bring in the person sending those threatening e-mails."

Reading between the lines wasn't difficult. "It's not Georgie, if that's what you're thinking," Clay informed him. There wasn't so much as an inch of room left for an argument. That settled, Clay shifted his attention back to his sister. "Who stole your money?" he inquired.

It was obvious that whoever it was, the man or woman was going to be in a hell of a lot of trouble once Clay tracked him or her down. Clay did not take kindly to anyone messing with his family. And since he'd washed his hands of Ryder when his younger brother had been sent to prison for sneaking illegal aliens over the border, that left only Georgie—and Emmie.

"I don't know," Georgie answered, doing her best not to let the distress show in her voice. She glanced at Nick as she spoke. "But they think it's me. On both counts."

"You?" he retorted incredulously. "You been traipsing around, following that damn rodeo for the last five months, living out of your trailer like some gypsy." He looked over at the stranger to make sure he'd gotten all that. "Just when the hell were you supposed to have done all this?"

Georgie looked at Nick again. "You have the dates the e-mails were sent, right?"

The petite, incredibly feisty woman had succeeded in

doing what no one else had in recent memory. She'd made him feel foolish even though he was just doing his job.

"On every one of the e-mails," he replied without a shred of emotion.

"My sister doesn't have the time for that kind of stupid nonsense," Clay told him tersely. "I don't think she even knows how to send an e-mail. For the last five months she was too busy trying to win trophies."

"Prize money, Clay," Georgie corrected, annoyed.

How many times did she have to tell him she didn't care about the accolades, the glory part? There was a very practical reason why she'd done what she had. Because competing in rodeo events was all she knew. She'd been put on a horse before she could walk and both her grandfather and her mother had been rodeo legends in their time. Rodeoing was in her genes.

Besides, it was the fastest way she knew to make money. Hell, it was the *only* way she knew how to make money.

"I was trying to win prize money so that Emmie and I could stay put here and she could go to school like a regular little girl come the fall." She glanced down fondly at her daughter.

"I'm not a regular little girl," Emmie interjected with protest, wrinkling her nose with disdain. Fisting her hands, she dug them into her hips the way she'd seen her mother do countless times.

"I know that, sweetie," Georgie told her, kissing the top of her daughter's head, "but we don't want the other kids to hear that. They'll be jealous."

Emmie nodded, understanding. Georgie bit her tongue to not laugh.

"You could have done that without risking breaking

every bone in your body," Clay told her. He'd been after her to quit the moment she'd told him she was going to compete. A lot of things could happen to a woman on the road with only a kid. "I would have been happy to give you the money."

They'd been through all this before. More than once. "I don't want to take your money, Clay."

Clay threw up his hands in frustration. "A loan, then. Damn it all, Georgie, what's my money good for if I can't do what I want with it?" he demanded.

Georgie patted him on the shoulder, the way she used to when she'd tried to calm him down and keep his sun-tanned complexion from turning a bright red.

"I'm sure that you'll find something else to do with it, big brother," she answered. And then she eyed him squarely, her lighter tone changing. "I don't want to be beholden to anyone, Clay, not even you. I'm my own person. If I take money from you, that changes everything."

He didn't see how. Damn it all, Georgie could still frustrate him the way no other woman could. "I'm not buying you, Georgie. I'm not even renting you. I just want to help."

"You can help by coming to Emmie's birthday party next week," she told him brightly, winking at her daughter.

Finding an in, Emmie was quick to try to further her own agenda. "You can buy me a pony, Uncle Clay. I won't give it back."

Again he laughed, this time the sound was softer. "Nice to know one of the women in the family has some sense," Clay told the little girl with affection. His eyes shifted toward Nick and the warmth abruptly evaporated. Clay looked the man up and down. "You some kind of government man?" he inquired.

"He's a Secret Service agent," Emmie was quick to inform him, enunciating the occupation carefully so as not to get it wrong.

Clay's eyes swept over the other man again. He would have pegged him for a member of the FBI or CIA instead. "Oh. You're a long way from home, Secret Service agent. Aren't you supposed to be guarding the President or something?"

"During an election year, we're assigned to the presidential candidates," Nick explained patiently, even though it was against his nature to explain himself at all. But being a stranger and alone here, he began to think he needed all the support he could get. "And someone's been sending threatening letters from your sister's house to the Senator." How many times was he going to have to repeat that story before he could finally leave? he wondered in frustration.

"You got somebody house-sitting?" he asked his sister. Georgie shook her head. "Then someone broke in."

She rolled her eyes. Didn't any man ever listen? "I already told you that."

Clay made up his mind. "That does it. You're getting your things and staying with me, both of you." For his money, they didn't even have to bother to pack. He could send one of hands to do the packing for her. "I've got the bigger place, anyway."

"You've got the much bigger place," Georgie acknowledged, "But that's not the point."

He might have known she was going to argue about this. Nothing came easy when it came to Georgie. "And what is the point, Georgie? Besides the one on top of your head, of course?"

She ignored the dig. Clay was just being frustrated because he knew he couldn't win. "The point is my home is here and nobody is going to run me off it."

He could admire bravery—when it came to someone else, not his sister, not his niece. "You've got Emmie to think of," he pointed out. "What if whoever broke in decides to come back?"

"Then I'll apprehend them," Nick told him, wedging himself into the conversation.

Clay looked at him coldly, as if he'd forgotten about his existence. "And just how to do you intend to do that?"

"By staying here until I can get to the bottom of this," Nick told Georgie's brother. It was obvious that the answer was not to the other man's liking.

Indignation blazed in Clay's dark eyes. "You're not staying here," he informed Nick.

Okay, enough with the big protector, Georgie thought. She got in between the two men. "This is my place, Clay," she reminded him. "I get to say who stays and who goes. And if I want Sheffield to stay here, then he stays here. My decision, not yours."

Judging by the other man's expression, Nick wouldn't have been able to say who was more surprised by her statement, her brother or him. He was tempted to ask her just when he had become part of the home team instead of someone she wanted to get rid of, but he knew to leave well enough alone.

Because of the present complexity of the situation and the doubts that had arisen in his own mind as to her culpability, he had planned to remain here, at the apparent starting point of the e-mails, until this was all resolved—or until he managed to catch Georgie Grady in a glaring lie—he wasn't completely convinced of her innocence. But one way or the other, he intended to get some answers.

Clay sighed. "You always were pig-headed."

Georgie flashed a particularly wide smile for Clay's benefit. "Nice to know that you can count on some things staying the same, right?"

Clay didn't answer. He didn't like the idea of some D.C. government spook watching over his sister. After all, she was nothing to the man. Besides, what if the other man started getting ideas about Georgie? Ideas that had nothing to do with e-mails and everything to do with the fact that his sister was a damn pretty woman.

Clay slipped his hands into his front pockets, rocking back on his boot heels. "I can hang around for a while if you want," he offered.

"You've got a ranch to run," she answered. "A successful ranch," she added. They might have their differences and she resisted his taking charge of her life, but she was proud of her brother and what he had accomplished despite the odds against him. "And I'm a little old to be needing a babysitter."

Clay didn't bother to hide his scorn of Nick. He trusted the Secret Service agent about as far as he could throw him. Less. "I wasn't thinking of you just now."

Since Sheffield had said he was going to try to help her, Georgie felt the need to apologize for Clay's behavior. "You've got to excuse my brother. He's used to being in charge of everything, whether we wanted him to be or not."

Clay took instant umbrage. "You don't have to make excuses for me to a stranger."

The last thing Nick wanted was to be in the middle of a family fight. "I assure you, all I'm interested in is finding out who sent those e-mails."

"And in getting back Mama's money," Emmie reminded him. When he looked down at her, she continued, "Remember? You said that in the bank, that you were going to get back her money."

Even Clay had to laugh at Emmie's interjection. "Don't say anything around half-pint you don't want coming back to haunt you. She doesn't forget a thing. And I mean *nothing*."

Nick looked to Georgie for guidance. "Are most kids her age like that?"

"Most kids *any* age aren't like that," Georgie told him. Draping her arm over the girl's shoulders, she gave her a quick squeeze. "Emmie's one of a kind."

"Unique," Emmie declared, gazing up at her mother. It was obvious that she liked the sound of the word.

Clay ruffled his niece's hair. "That's right, half-pint. Unique." He paused for a moment to turn to his sister. His expression softened. "You sure I can't talk you into coming over to my place and staying there for a few days?"

"I'm sure." Maybe, if things got worse, she'd taken him up on his offer. But right now, she wanted to face this on her own. "You're within hollering range, big brother," she told him cheerfully. "I'll holler if I need you."

"Yeah, right." She was too proud. He didn't believe her for a minute. "When pigs fly."

Georgie grinned, amused. "Definite right after that, I promise."

Clay addressed Nick. "See that nothing happens to

either of them, Secret Service agent. I'm holding you personally responsible if it does." Not that there was much comfort in that, he thought.

"Don't worry, Mr. Grady," Nick assured him. "It won't."

Clay's expression darkened instantly. "The name's not Grady."

Confused, Nick shifted his eyes to Georgie before looking back at her older brother. "Your sister said she wasn't married, so I just assumed that Grady was the family name."

"It is," Clay told him, then added, "Our mother's family."

Taking pity on him, Georgie began to explain, "My grandfather was a rodeo star—"

"Like my grandma," Emmie piped up with pride. George "Rattlesnake" Grady had died before she was born, but her mother's stories had made the man seem vividly real to the little girl.

Clay doled out his words slowly. "Grady was their last name."

Georgie picked up the thread. "I took it as my stage name." Nick felt as if he was suddenly a spectator at a tennis match. "To keep the family tradition alive." That was apparently as much as she was willing to share at the moment. Turning on her heel, she faced her brother. It was obvious that she was dismissing him even though she'd been the one to ask him to come over to begin with. Calling on a woman's prerogative, she'd had a change of heart. "I'll call you if anything comes up."

Clay didn't look as if he believed her for a moment. "Yeah."

"I promise," Georgie repeated earnestly. "You'll be the first to know."

Emmie tugged on her shirt, her lower lip stuck out like a little perch. "Not me, Mama?"

She grinned. No matter how awful she felt, Emmie always managed to cheer her up, just by being there. "All right, Uncle Clay will be the second to know." She looked up at her brother. "Good enough?" she asked him.

Clay snorted. As if he had a say in this. It was like trying to win an argument with a rock. "Guess it'll have to be."

"Give your uncle a kiss, Emmie," Georgie urged, gently pushing the girl toward Clay. "One of your butterfly specials. That'll cheer him up."

Okay, he'd bite, Nick thought. "What's a butterfly special?"

Before Georgie could explain, Emmie turned toward him. "I'll show you," the little girl volunteered. She tugged on his jacket. "Well, c'mon. You've gotta bend down."

Feeling awkward, Nick did as the little girl instructed and bent down to her level. She leaned forward and he felt the slight brush of her small, rosebud lips against his cheek. And then there was something more. Just the slightest sensation. He realized that Emmie had turned her face slightly and she was fluttering her eyelashes against his skin, just above where she'd kissed him.

Something warm and nameless materialized within his chest and spread.

Giggling, Emmie danced away on tiptoes, moving toward her next target: Clay. "Your turn, Uncle Clay. Bend down."

He did and she repeated the brief performance. And

then, backing away from her uncle, again on tiptoes, Emmie steepled her small fingers in front of her mouth to hold back another pleased giggle. It escaped anyway. Her laughter was infectious as it filled the air.

"Now I'm good to go," Clay told her, straightening. The smile left his lips as he raised his head and regarded Nick one last time. "*You* call me if anything comes up," he ordered. "She probably won't." He nodded his head toward his sister.

"All right." It was neither a promise nor lip service. Calling the other man was something he would consider doing or not doing when and if the time came. "By the way," he began, remembering a lost thread of the conversation. He fell into step with the man as the latter headed toward his parked truck.

Georgie and Emmie stood where they were left, watching and, in Emmie's case, waving.

Clay didn't even bother turning around to look at the man addressing him. "Yeah?"

"What is your last name?" Nick asked. "Just for the record."

Clay didn't pause until he'd reached his truck. Then he turned and gave him one last long measuring glance. Clay laughed, shaking his head. There was very little humor in the sound. If Nick listened closely, he would have noted a touch of irony.

"You government types do like to keep your 'records' straight, don't you?" Clay mocked. "Okay, 'just for the record,' Sheffield, it's Colton. Clay Colton. Colton, in case you're wondering, was the name of the no-good, worthless excuse of a man who thought my mother was good enough to warm his sheets, and have his bastards, but wasn't good enough to marry."

With that, Clay got into his truck, leaving Nick to stare after him in stunned silence. The name Clay had just uttered echoed over and over again inside Nick's head.

Colton.

Chapter 9

Nick turned away from the road. Georgie and her daughter were on the steps of the front porch, about to enter the house. He addressed the back of her head.

"Why didn't you tell me your last name was Colton?"

His question stopped her for a moment, but then she continued walking. She didn't bother to turn around. "You never asked."

He followed her into the house. This wasn't some abstract conversation they were having, this had direct bearing on the reason he was down here and he meant to get to the bottom of it.

Had everything she'd told him up to now been a lie, after all?

"Don't give me that. Seems to me that only a guilty person would have kept that kind of information back."

Georgie kept going until she came to the kitchen. Although she knew the state of affairs within her refrigerator—empty—she opened it anyway, just to confirm that her mystery squatter hadn't left behind any food.

"How about a person who doesn't share things that are nobody else's business but their own?" She closed the refrigerator door a little harder than she needed to and squared her shoulders in an unconscious, defensive movement. Her eyes narrowed. "I don't see you telling me about your parents, or lack thereof."

She added the latter as she thought of her absentee father. The one she'd never met or even heard from—until just recently. For some reason, out of the blue, Graham Colton had materialized, saying he wanted to make amends for his past behavior. Had her mother been alive, she would have tried to find the good in the man, but her mother was gone. The time for mending fences was long gone. She was doing just fine without having the man in her life at this stage. And she intended to continue that way.

Nick set his jaw hard as he pointed out the obvious. "I'm not the one sending threatening e-mails to a United States Senator."

Georgie whirled around on her heel, her hands fisted at her waist to keep from taking a swing at this infuriating man.

"Well, funny you should say that because neither am I and the sooner you get that through your thick head, the sooner both of us will be happy and you can be on your way."

Gleaning what she needed to from her mother's words, Emmie turned her big green eyes up to the man in the black suit. "You're not gonna help my mama?"

Nick had never spent much time dealing with children. Consequently, he had no idea what to make of them and it had been so long since he'd even *had* a childhood. But he knew hurt when he saw it. He knew an accusatory tone when he heard it, and Emmie Grady—or Colton—was wielding both like a well-trained samurai swinging his sword.

Georgie draped her arm protectively over the little girl's slim shoulders. "He's gonna help mama by leaving, baby," she told her daughter. Looking at Nick, she said, "There's your hat, there's your car, what's your hurry?" uttering the ironic line to usher him along on his way. She might have known better.

"No hurry," he responded, then regarded Emmie, "And yes, I'm going to help your mama." Because, he added silently, this all somehow went together.

To his surprise, Emmie took his hand and began to pull him toward the living room, her small face a wreath of smiles. "I knew you would."

Georgie sighed. Maybe Emmie saw some good in him she was missing. At any rate, she seemed to be stuck with the man for a while. Yes, she'd told her brother that Sheffield could stay at her place, but that was just to restore her independence, her authority over herself in case Clay wanted to institute some form of martial law over her life. She'd silently hoped that Sheffield would leave once her brother did. No such luck, it seemed.

"I suppose you'll be wanting lunch."

"Eventually," Nick allowed. And then he realized what she was saying. He eyed her sharply. "Don't bother yourself. I'll go into town and grab something to eat. You do have a restaurant in Esperanza, right?"

She thought of the one where her mother had worked all those long hours after giving up her career on the rodeo circuit. The rodeo had been her mother's first love, but she had given it all up for them, for Clay, Ryder and her, to give them a stable home life. Georgie couldn't help wondering if her mother had ever regretted what she'd done.

She had a feeling she knew the answer.

"Yes, we have a restaurant in Esperanza, a damn decent one, too, but I've got to go back into town to get some food for Emmie and me. I might as well feed you, too," she told him.

Georgie was annoyed with herself for not tending to that, too, when she'd gone into town earlier. But discovering that she was flat broke had made her forget the basics. Like the importance of stocking her pantry and refrigerator.

It was time she got a grip on herself and started functioning like the independent woman she was, not like some scatterbrained woman she wasn't.

Grabbing the keys she'd left on the table, Georgie gestured toward her daughter. "C'mon, Emmie, we've got to go back into town."

Emmie surprised both her mother and Nick with her next words. "Can I stay with Nick, Mama?"

"That's Mr. Sheffield, honey," Georgie corrected. Emmie called the cowboys on the circuit by their first names, but that was different. Those were men who doted on her. This was an agent of the government. "And I'm sure he's got a whole bunch of things he wants to do that don't include babysitting a little girl."

Her request completely mystified Nick. "Why would you want to stay with me?"

"'Cause I've got questions to ask you," Emmie told him solemnly.

Had Emmie been older, he would have suspected a setup, with Georgie putting words into the child's mouth. But Emmie looked too young to be a shill, even for her mother. "Questions?"

Emmie nodded, her red curls bouncing like thin springs about her head. "Like how do those go on?" Before he could ask what she was referring to, Emmie pointed a small index finger at the handcuffs hanging off his belt. Usually hidden by his jacket, the garment had gotten stuck on them, exposing just enough steel to capture Emmie's attention.

Georgie took hold of Emmie's hand and began to lead her to the front door. "Careful what you wish for, honey. He just might show you," she murmured under her breath, but loud enough for both Emmie *and* Nick to hear.

It suddenly occurred to him that there was an advantage to having the little girl remain. Moving quickly, he shifted himself in front of mother and daughter before they could reach the front door. "She can stay."

Georgie looked up at him and read between the lines. The man was pretty transparent. "Don't worry, I'll be back. You don't need a hostage," she told him deliberately.

She took a step to get around him. He took one to keep in front of her. "If Emmie stays here, I'll be sure of it."

Did he think she was born yesterday? Or did he just think she was that stupid? "I'm not leaving my four-year-old daughter alone with a man I don't know."

"Five, Mama, I'm almost five," Emmie reminded her, holding up five splayed fingers.

Nick ignored the little girl. "Fair enough," he

allowed. He'd set about as many wheels in motion as he could right now. This could come under the heading of surveillance work. "I guess we're going grocery shopping then."

The only one who seemed happy about the arrangement was Emmie, who suddenly threaded her tiny fingers through Nick's while still holding on to her mother's hand. Positioned between them, she gleefully proclaimed, "Just like a real family."

It took everything Nick had not to yank his hand away.

The ache the words created within Georgie's chest was immeasurable.

I can't give you that now, Emmie. But maybe someday, she promised. *Maybe someday.*

"Careful, honey, or you're going to give Mr. Sheffield a heart attack," she said flippantly. "He'd probably got a wife and kids at home."

Never one to hold back, Emmie took her question to the source. "Do you?" Emmie pressed, twisting around to get a better look at Nick's face as he dropped back a step.

Reaching the truck, Georgie picked up her daughter and slipped her into the car seat, securing the belts. All the while Emmie craned her neck, watching Nick and waiting for an answer.

"No," he answered in a monotone. "I don't." Getting into the cab of the truck, he waited for Georgie to climb in on her side and give him the keys. There was no way he was allowing the woman to drive. There'd be no telling where they would wind up if he did.

The shopping expedition into town took a little less than two hours, start to finish.

At the checkout counter, after everything had been

tallied, Georgie reached for one of her credit cards, then remembered that she'd canceled them all. That left her dependent on cash until the companies issued her new cards and sent them.

Murmuring an apology, Georgie dug into her wallet for cash. Nick elbowed her out of the way and handed the checker a hundred dollar bill.

"That should cover it," he said.

The young woman behind the counter looked barely out of high school. She regarded the bill with suspicion as she held it up to the light, angling it as if she expected to see the word "counterfeit' written across the back.

So much for trust, Nick thought, mildly amused at another stereotype biting the dust. "It's real," he assured her.

The young blonde flushed. "We don't see many of these," she responded, handing him change with what could only be described as an inviting smile.

"You didn't have to pay for it," Georgie protested, pushing the cart out of the store.

"You don't have to cook for me," he countered, keeping step. Emmie had wound her fingers around his left hand again, all but skipping alongside him and her mother.

You'd think Emmie would have better judgment than that, Georgie thought. She was about to make a cryptic comment about cooking for him, then sighed. She had to think of Emmie and set a good example. So she nodded and said, "Fair enough, I guess."

He surprised her by loading the grocery bags into the truck, then picking up Emmie and depositing her into her car seat. Allowing him to buckle in Emmie, she still checked to see that the belts were secure.

"Would you like to redo them?" he asked.

"Just making sure she's secure. I don't expect you've had much experience with kids' car seats."

"A seat belt's a seat belt," he responded. "You want to drive?" he asked, holding out the keys.

She was about to snatch them away. The keys and the truck that went with them represented her independence. But then she shrugged. She didn't want to do what he expected her to do.

"You can drive," she told him, climbing into the passenger seat.

She missed the smile that curved the corners of his mouth just before he got in.

After he'd helped Georgie and Emmie bring in the grocery bags, it dawned on him. Power had been restored to the house, just as Georgie had foretold last night. That meant that he could get back to working on her computer in an effort to see if he had missed something the first time around, before the power from the portable generator had given out.

"I'm going to get back to working on your computer," he told her as he began to leave the kitchen. "Whoever stole your identity might have been using it to do their 'shopping' with your credit cards."

"What do you hope to find?" she asked. She couldn't begin to fathom using the machine as a tracking device, but then, she'd be the first to admit that she was naive in the ways of computers.

"I don't know yet," he admitted.

"Well, that's not very encouraging."

"Most clues turn up by accident," he told her, leaving the room.

"Definitely not encouraging," she murmured under

her breath. Pushing everything else out of her mind, she turned her attention to making lunch. Specifically, to making burritos. Mexican food always made her feel better and she really needed something to make her feel better.

Left to her own devices, Emmie decided that now would be as good a time as any for "Mr. Sheffield" to answer those questions buzzing in her head. Slipping out of the kitchen, she came bounding into her mother's bedroom.

"Hi," she declared cheerfully. Not standing on ceremony, or hanging back, she planted herself beside him at the card table.

Nick looked up. Lost in thought for a moment, he'd forgotten about the little girl.

"Hi," he murmured and, inadvertently, opened the door for her. The questions came, fast and furious, as to how his handcuffs worked. Why did he need them? Did he see many bad people? What did he do when he saw them? And on and on. There seemed to be no end in sight, her fertile mind coming up with question after question.

Emmie only stopped to draw breath when he chose to answer a question. She distracted him to the point that he eventually placed what he was doing on hold. He'd found what he was looking for, at least to some extent. Unearthing user history, he found a score of places that had been hit, all online stores. Unlike Georgie, whoever had used this computer had a log-on user name and password for each site. He was going to have to get Steve hooked up to the computer in order to ascertain them. He had a feeling that if he found the names, he'd find the person sending the threatening e-mails as well.

God, he hoped he wasn't being taken for a ride—by two redheads.

"Lunch is ready, you two." Standing in the doorway to her bedroom, Georgie repeated what she'd first called out from the kitchen, getting no response. It seemed that her daughter and her uninvited "guest" hadn't heard her so rather than call again, she decided to just fetch them and be done with it.

She hadn't expected to find them kneeling on the floor on opposite sides of her bed. Especially not Sheffield.

Georgie looked from her daughter to the man who had summarily invaded her life and turned everything within it upside down. She decided that she'd get a better answer from Emmie than from Sheffield.

"Just what in the name of all that's sacred are you doing, Emmie?" she asked, addressing the top of the little girl's head—it was all that was peeking out from the far side of her bed.

Emmie popped up, grinning and looking very pleased with herself. "Playing cops and robbers, Mama. I'm the cop."

Georgie turned to see the Secret Service agent on his knees, handcuffs securely on his wrists and an exceedingly sheepish look on his face. "I guess that must make you the robber." She didn't bother struggling to keep the amused expression from her face.

Silently declaring the game to be over, he rose to his feet. "Yeah." He thrust his bound hands before him and at Georgie. "Get these off me." The widening grin on her face did not fill him full of confidence.

"Not so fast," Georgie drawled. "I think I like having you handcuffed."

But Emmie was already making her way to her new playmate. "But he can't eat if he's handcuffed, Mama," she said, the soul of logic. Taking the key she'd placed in her pocket, Emmie inserted it into the lock and turned it.

Handcuffs unlocked, Nick quickly removed them from his wrists, still not entirely sure how he'd allowed himself to get "captured" in the first place.

"I know," Georgie agreed, "But he'd be a lot less trouble that way."

Rubbing his wrists, Nick temporarily deposited the handcuffs into his pocket. "You know the penalty for falsely imprisoning a Secret Service Agent?" he asked Georgie.

Georgie turned her face up to his innocently. "Peace and quiet?" she ventured.

He had no idea why, but he had this overwhelming urge to kiss the grin off her lips. Had to be all this fresh air, he theorized. It was obviously doing strange things to his head.

"Get a move on," Georgie ordered. He wasn't sure if it was aimed at him, or her daughter, or both. "The food's getting cold." She led the way back. Nick did his best to keep his eyes fixed on the back of Georgie's head rather than on the way her hips swayed in her tight jeans as she walked.

The rest of the day was spent less pleasantly, spinning his wheels, making very little headway, although Steve told him that he would do his best to hack into Georgie's computer and get past the encrypted passwords. Nightfall came before he knew it.

Emmie seemed to finally run out of energy and had to be carried off to bed, sound asleep. Something stirred within him as he watched Georgie carry her daughter to her room. For some reason, the extremely domestic scene got to him and started him thinking. Wondering about the road not taken.

And then he shook off those thoughts. He wasn't interested in that road, he reminded himself. He would have been bored within the first day.

But watching Georgie Grady/Colton now, he had to admit that there was something going on. It was the "what" that remained unidentified to him.

Careful, Nicky, he warned himself. *You don't want to be making any mistakes now.*

He was human and he'd been conned before. But never by anyone nearly so attractive. Never by anyone he'd felt so attracted to.

In her defense, Nick supposed that Georgie could actually be telling him the truth. That she was a victim in all this. He had Steve checking all that out for him, checking her out, to make sure she was who she said she was and had, as she claimed, not even been near a computer these last few months.

In the meantime, he thought cryptically, he was doing his own checking out. Up close and exceedingly personal. So personal, he could feel his blood stirring.

It had been a long time since he'd thought of himself as anything other than a law enforcement agent of one type or other. But Georgeann Grady made him remember that beneath the oaths he had taken and the extreme devotion to duty he felt, there beat the heart of a man.

A man who'd been far too long without the touch of a woman.

The power was on, but she seemed to prefer having the fire in the fireplace lit. He watched now as the light from the fireplace caressed the outline of Georgie's small, trim, jean-clad body. She moved about the rustic living room that could have easily come off the set of a Hollywood western. Except that it was genuine.

As genuine as she claimed to be?

Something inside him hoped so.

Not very professional of you, Nicky.

He wasn't supposed to be taking sides. His only interest in being here was to guarantee Senator Joe Colton's safety as the latter continued to make his bid for the presidency. Everything else was supposed to be secondary.

But, Nick had to silently admit, that was just a wee bit hard to remember right now.

Earlier, before she'd put her precocious handful of a daughter to bed, Georgie had fed his appetite by whipping up some kind of a delicious concoction out of the vegetables she'd pulled from her garden. Vegetables that, by all rights, should have been withered and dried. She'd mentioned that a friend came by on occasion to weed and tend the garden. Still, it surprised him that somehow she'd managed to make something mouth-watering out of very little.

Almost as mouth-watering as she looked to him right then.

Again, he was reminded of the appetite that hadn't been fed, hadn't been satisfied.

And wasn't going to be, Nick sternly told himself. At least, not now. Maybe when things took on a more definite shape and all the questions in his head were, once and for all, answered to his satisfaction, there would be time to explore this feeling. To explore this woman. But not now.

Damn it.

"I can turn the lights back up," Georgie said, breaking into his train of thought as she turned around to face him. If she noticed the way he was looking at her, she gave no indication. "But Emmie wanted to pretend that we were still roughing it. This way, she could pretend we were camping out. Emmie really likes to camp out."

"And you?" Nick asked, moving closer. "What do you like?"

The very breath stopped in Georgie's throat as she looked up at him.

And then, all sorts of things ricocheted in her head.

Things that didn't make sense.

Things that had to do with needs rather than the logical behavior she had been trying so hard to embrace for the last few hours.

"I think you've got a fair shot of guessing that one," she told him softly.

Chapter 10

Nick was acutely aware that he was crossing a line. A line he had never ventured over before in his adult life.

His action was reminiscent of the rebellious youth he'd been rather than the man he had carefully and painstakingly evolved into. The man would have never given in to the moment, to the temptation shimmering before him.

No matter how much he wanted to.

But it was the rebellious teen, who hadn't quite figured out how to harness himself, how to tame his impulses, who surfaced.

Nick cupped the sides of Georgie's face in his hands and brought his mouth down to hers as if he had no choice in the matter. And it was that needy soul, the one who had never connected with anyone after his mother's desertion, who silently cheered as sensations shot through him, causing him to deepen the kiss that was far from innocent.

My God, what's going on?

The shell-shocked question echoed in Georgie's brain before it showered down on her in shattered fragments. Before she embraced the wild feelings that had materialized out of nowhere. When Nick kissed her, she voluntarily fell headlong into it, losing herself. She could sooner stop breathing than pull back.

The ensuing rush was incredible.

It had been so long since she'd allowed a man to kiss her. The last few years, she'd lived her life almost exclusively in the world of men, but they were her friends, her mentors, her protectors. They looked out for her almost as if she were a beloved little sister. Once or twice, a new member had joined the circle and attempted to hit on her. But there was always someone to set the newcomer straight and he would obligingly back off.

As far as the men on the rodeo circuit were concerned, Georgie was family. Her boundaries were to be respected and not crossed.

And she had gone along, silently grateful for the protection, for being left alone on the complex romantic playing field.

She thought she was all right with that. She thought wrong.

This need that had sprung up from nowhere, exploding like a misstep taken in an active minefield, had to have had its origins somewhere, didn't it?

The more Nick kissed her, the more she wanted to be kissed. The more she realized how much she'd missed being kissed, being treated like a desirable woman rather than just a mother, just a sister, just a worthy competitor. There was nothing wrong with any of that, but it didn't begin to address the needs that had quietly been growing in the dark. Growing until they burst at the seams.

He should pull back.

He should get a grip and stop. *Now,* before he compounded the mistake.

But the feel of her soft body urgently pressing against his had set off all sorts of demands within him that were close to impossible to rein in.

He tried to talk himself out of it, using logic. It could all be just part of her plan to seduce him, to turn his head and make him oblivious to her guilt, to the con she wanted to put over on him.

God help him, he didn't care.

He'd sort it all out later. Right now, something far more important was going on. And besides, deep in his gut, he felt she was innocent. That was supposed to count for something, wasn't it? Gut feelings?

Or was he just trying to rationalize his behavior?

Breath short, pulse racing and adrenaline pumped up so high he thought he was about to plunge off the side of a cliff into a glass of water three hundred feet below, Nick still somehow managed to break contact and pull his head back.

Somehow managed to pull his lips away from hers. "Georgie—"

That's all he said. That's all he could say. Because she rose up on her toes, whispered a plea, "Don't ruin this," and sealed her mouth to his as she drove her fingers into his hair, anchoring herself to the sensation that thundered through her.

It was all he needed. The go-ahead signal. Had he been made of cardboard or metal, he could have called a stop to it. But he was flesh and blood and his flesh and blood called to hers.

As he tightened his arms around her, his mouth roamed Georgie's face, her neck, the soft skin that peered out from where the first button of her blouse pulled against its hole.

As he kissed her, his mouth doing wild, wonderful things to her system she'd never experienced, Georgie felt his fingers freeing the buttons on her blouse.

And then her blouse was hanging open, exposing her lacy bra and showing off her tanned, firm skin to its best advantage.

His lips anointed her skin.

With unsteady hands, Georgie began to undress him, first pushing the damn black jacket off his shoulders, down his arms, then setting siege to his shirt. She yanked the edges out of his waistband, but as she began to free the buttons, she felt herself being picked up into the air.

Startled, she looked at Nick, a silent question in her eyes.

"Your daughter might wake up," he told her, his voice husky with emotions that had yet to be spent.

Oh, God, Emmie. She'd forgotten about Emmie.

If she'd been thinking clearly, she would have been embarrassed that he was the one who thought of Emmie. After all, she was Emmie's mother. But Georgie was grateful that he knew Emmie could come out of her room at any time, looking for her. Her heart swelled and an incredible wave of tenderness washed over her. That one simple act made her see him in a completely different light.

Again she sealed her mouth to his, kissing him long

and hard. The only reason she broke contact was because he was depositing her on her bed.

And then he was helping her out of her jeans, pulling them down about her thighs and then her knees. His own knees felt almost weak as she raised her hips to help with the effort. Raised them so that they were closer to him.

Tossing the jeans aside on the floor, Nick reached for the soft, light blue bikini panties she still had on. Meanwhile, she had tangled her fingers in his belt, drawing it quickly through its loops. She didn't even wait to have it hit the floor before she yanked on the zipper.

The button that fastened the trousers in place went flying. Momentarily distracted, Nick glanced to see where it had landed.

Georgie pulled his face back down to hers. "I can sew," she told him just before she captured his mouth again.

She desperately wanted nothing to stop her. If she paused, if she thought, logic and her sense of self-preservation would get in the way and stop her.

And she didn't want to stop.

She wanted to dash up to the highest pinnacle, to feel that rush through her veins just a moment before it was all over. She needed to feel that more than she could possibly ever put into words.

With a mighty tug, Georgie freed him of both his trousers and the underwear beneath them, bringing both down around his surprisingly muscular thighs and then off his torso completely. They fell into the shadows, along with the button.

"Learn that on the circuit?" he asked, trying to hide the desire that throbbed through his veins beneath a glimmer of humor.

"No," she whispered, her breath lingering on his

face, "but I could hog-tie you in a minute eight if you want a demonstration of what I did learn on the circuit."

He framed her face with his hands, drawing the length of his naked body over hers. "Later."

"Okay."

It was the last thing she remembered saying before everything exploded within her. Before he made her feel beautiful. Before her skin went on fire as he branded her with his hands, his mouth, his tongue.

Georgie swallowed strangled cries as he made her climax and then continued, doing it again.

And again.

Until she thought she was just going to expire from exhaustion.

With her last ounce of available strength, Georgie wrapped her legs around Nick's torso, stirring up temptation he couldn't resist, couldn't ignore or back away from.

Balancing his weight across his hands as if he were coming down from a powerful push-up, Nick plunged into her. A moment later, he was employing a rhythm that was older than time, and as new as the next second.

At the end, she would have cried out if his mouth hadn't covered hers. She arched up as far as she could, trying to absorb every last fragment of sensation and hug it to her breast.

Then she realized that he had stopped moving.

When he rolled off her the next moment, she expected Nick to get up. To act as if all of this was no big deal. The way Jason had. Jason was her only frame of reference, the only other man she had slept with.

That Nick didn't automatically get up surprised her. That he slipped his arm around her and drew her closer to him surprised her even more.

Almost as much as it surprised him.

He wanted to hang on to the sensation, to the exquisite moment, knowing that once it faded, there would be anger.

His own directed at himself.

Because he had slipped off the path he'd laid out for himself—slipped off big time. But just for a moment longer, he wanted to pretend that there were no consequences, that he had done nothing wrong. He'd simply enjoyed another human being.

He felt her turning her head toward him. Felt her studying him for a long, silent moment. And then she asked, "Did I just compromise you, or did you just compromise me?"

The question took him aback. So much so that he raised himself up on his elbow in order to look at down her. "What?"

Georgie blew out a long breath. "What just happened here?"

He grinned. The temptation to say that they'd just stood in the path of a twister was hard to resist. Instead, he teased her. "You are Emmie's biological mother, right?"

Georgie frowned as she shook her head. "I'm not talking about the process. I *know* what happened here, but," she looked up at him. "What happened here?"

She couldn't word it any better than that. Because something *had* happened here. Something unsettling and overwhelming.

Nick shrugged, trying his best to regain ground, to appear nonchalant. But underneath, he was wondering the same thing. He did his best to define it. "I think we just had a moment."

She glanced at her wristwatch. "It was a hell of a lot

longer than just a moment. More like an hour," she corrected.

He laughed then. And laughing beside her felt almost as good as making love with her.

It had been a long time since he'd laughed. Longer than the last time he'd allowed himself to make love to a woman.

His laugh was deep and rich, making her feel inherently good. Inherently happy.

"That's a nice sound," she told him, unconsciously curling her body into his. "You should laugh more often."

He thought of the life he had been leading. There was satisfaction, but no humor. "Not much to laugh at in my line of work," he responded.

"Your line of work," she echoed thoughtfully. And then she smiled to herself at the irony. "You mean catching bad guys like me?"

He looked at her for a long moment. Again, his instincts told him she was innocent. But there was the evidence to consider. Her IP address and her computer were involved in this. Logically, that would mean that she was too. *And* she had hidden her last name from him. Because she was accustomed to using her stage name, or because it made her look guilty?

"Tell me about your father," he finally said.

He felt her stiffen slightly against him, and then he saw her force herself to relax. "Is this how you conduct your second wave of interrogation? Naked?"

Nick shifted, pulling her toward him. His hand gently rested on the swell of her hip. He felt himself being aroused again. Something else out of the ordinary, he thought. Usually, when he got to this part, he'd be sated and that would be that.

Not this time.

"It does have its advantages." Maybe it was the moment, or the aftermath of lovemaking, but he leveled with her. "My gut tells me you're innocent—"

She didn't bother suppressing the smile that rose to her lips. "Your 'gut,' or something else?"

"My gut," he assured her. "But I need to be convinced a little more." A wary expression came into her eyes. He could guess at what she was thinking. That he was coaxing her to make love with him again. "No, not like that. Answer my question. Tell me about your father."

"Nothing to tell." Rather than look at him, Georgie stared off into space, doing her best to divorce herself from her words. She'd convinced herself that it didn't matter, that the years when she'd wanted her father were in her past. She'd gotten over that. But a part of her still hurt, still smarted from being abandoned along with her brothers and mother. And she would never forgive him for turning his back on her mother.

"He came into my mother's life, turned her whole world upside down, gave her three babies and then left. He went back to his rich wife. I never knew him when I was growing up, although Clay said he came around for a little while." She set her jaw hard as she continued. "Now he's back, trying to make amends. Probably because his own kids can't stand him from what I hear." She told him with no little feeling, "I've got no use for him."

This didn't sound like the Joe Colton he knew. Joe Colton was an honorable man. He would have never had an affair, especially not one that extended over several years' time. But to be thorough, he had to ask. "What's your father's first name?"

"Graham." She knew where he was going with this. "Don't worry, Secret Service Agent Sheffield, it's not your precious Senator. Just somebody with the same last name."

He watched her face. Unless she was one hell of an accomplished actress, he thought, she was telling the truth. "But you're all related."

"Maybe. But I don't care," she added truthfully. "I care about my immediate family. My daughter and my brothers." Ryder might have taken a few wrong turns that had landed him in prison, but he was still her brother and she loved him. There were ties that went beyond logic. "I care about the men I ride the rodeo circuit with," she told him. "And that's it. Oh, and I care about who's been impersonating me." She could see that the addition surprised him. And then she said with feeling, "Because I'm going to strangle her."

He laughed softly at first, then realized that there was no humor in her eyes. "You sound as if you mean that."

"Of course I mean it." As she spoke, her indignation at what the other woman had done grew like a flash fire. "She stole something precious from me."

Her life savings. He could understand her anger. "The money—"

But Georgie waved her hand at that. The money represented security and was exceedingly important, but something was more important to her. "That's secondary. She stole my good name. I don't know about where you come from, Sheffield, but around here, your good name, your word, means something."

A woman of integrity, he thought, nodding. But then he supposed he could expect nothing less of her, just from what he'd learned in the last twenty-four hours.

Georgie cleared her throat, feeling somewhat awkward. She was still naked, still lying beside a naked man and without her passion, which was spent, or her anger, which was slowly settling down, she felt uncomfortably vulnerable even though she couldn't exactly explain why.

"Um, don't you think you should get up and go to your bed in the guest room?"

"Right. Sure." And then, giving in to impulse, Nick lightly brushed his lips against her bare shoulder. Something began to stir within him again. "In a minute—or so."

Damn, there it went again, that blaze that he seemed to be able to ignite within her. She should be sated, for heaven's sake, and yet, she wanted more. She wanted to take another wild ride before the night was over. What had come over her?

"Are you starting up again?" she asked, turning her body to his. And then she smiled before he could answer—because another part of his body had answered her question for him. The smile entered her eyes and seemed to simply glow everywhere. "I guess so."

Damn but she was beautiful, he thought. "Anybody ever tell you you talk too much?"

She seemed to roll his question over in her mind, her smile widening as she did so, pulling him in. "You wouldn't be the first."

"I didn't think so." But something inside of him, as he brought his mouth down to hers again, whispered that he wanted to be the last. And telling Georgie she talked too much had nothing to do with it.

Chapter 11

In order to keep his word and satisfy Emmie, who popped up like toast the next morning to remind him of his promise to "make everything right for Mama," Nick spent the first part of his morning at Georgie's computer, tracking down all the charges incurred on her credit cards. Just to play it safe, armed with the user names and passwords Steve had sent him, Nick decided to go back over the last five months.

One by one, he secured the information, then printed it out for her. When he had the charges in a rather overwhelming stack, he gave the pages to her and left it up to Georgie to decipher, separating the piles into charges she had run up and the ones that could be attributed to the "Georgie" doppelganger.

Having lived up to his part of the bargain, Nick got down to his real work. He decided that it might be advantageous to find out as much as he could about the man who had fathered Georgie and her brothers, the mysterious and, from what he'd gathered, self-centered Graham Colton.

It took some digging at first, but once he had some key pieces of information to work with, the rest came more easily.

An hour after he'd gotten started, hopping from screen to screen and from site to site, he found himself staring at the information the winding trail had brought him to. And discovering something he would have rather not found out.

Because what he'd found out unearthed another battery of questions and, more importantly, doubts.

Away from Georgie and the attraction he experienced whenever he was within ten feet of her, Nick felt uncertainty taking root again.

Had he been played?

Or was there some outside chance that she actually didn't know that her father, Graham Colton, was the Senator's younger brother? After all, not even he had known that the Senator had a younger brother, much less what his name was.

But then, Graham Colton wasn't *his* father. Wouldn't Georgie have connected the dots? Or was politics something she blocked out, the way so many other people did? After all, it wasn't as if Graham Colton had been a doting father. All the evidence he'd come across so far pointed to the fact that he'd been, probably still was, a womanizing, narcissistic, greedy scum. In Georgie's place, he wouldn't have wanted to have anything to do with the man either. But did not wanting contact mean ignorance of his family background?

He wasn't sure.

With a sigh, Nick stretched out his legs beneath the table, debating his next move. What he'd just found out wasn't something he could keep to himself.

But if he told Georgie, one of two things could happen. If she didn't know, this would be a hell of a shock for her. And if she did know and had lied to him, he wasn't certain how he'd deal with that particular scenario.

He supposed that he could hold off telling her. There was time enough to discover whether he'd made love with an innocent or a scheming witch. He'd just begun to entertain illusions, he didn't want to have to risk losing them already.

There was one person he did have to tell. The one person who deserved to be apprised of anything he found out as soon as possible.

Nick shifted in his chair, sitting up straight again as he took his cell phone out of his pocket. He pressed the single button that would connect him to the Senator's private cell.

Waiting, Nick counted off four rings before he heard the sound of a phone coming to life on the other end of the line. A dynamic, resonant voice said, "Hello?"

Even the man's voice inspired him with confidence, Nick thought. "Senator Colton, this is Nick Sheffield."

"Nick." Pleasure flooded the Senator's voice. "I was just wondering when I'd be hearing from you. I was beginning to get concerned that you decided to forget about the campaign and just settle in." There was almost a wistful note in his tone. "Awfully pretty country down there."

"If you like the rustic life," Nick responded, not quite able to get himself to agree to the Senator's assessment. He was just *not* the rural type. Nick was fairly certain that his voice gave him away on that count. "I'm calling because I found where the e-mails were coming from."

The Senator immediately heard what wasn't being said. "But not the person sending them?"

No doubt about it, Nick thought. The Senator was quick on the uptake. "Well, there seems to be some doubt about it," he told the man. "The woman whose computer was used to send the e-mails was out of town during the period of time we've blocked off."

"Is someone else in the family doing the sending, then?"

"I'm looking into that," Nick told the man. Uncomfortable with what he was about to say, he shifted in his seat. "Senator, there's something else."

"Go on."

There was no easy way to say this. Since the Senator didn't talk about his brother, Nick assumed that there was bad blood between them. Or hard feelings. The Senator was a successful, powerful, well-liked man. Maybe his brother, who hadn't seemed to have amounted to very much in his lifetime, was resentful of his success. "The woman's last name's Colton. Graham Colton's her father."

"It was Georgie's computer that was being used to send the e-mails?" Joe asked, surprised.

So much for catching the man off guard. But then, that was part of what he admired about the Senator. The man was as savvy as they came and literally seemed to be on top of everything. No one had ever managed to catch him sleeping.

"You know about her, sir?"

"Yes. And about her brothers, Clay and Ryder, as well. I know all about my brother's other family, Nick." Nick thought he heard a stifled sigh on the other end. "Proud woman, Mary Lynn. After Graham had deserted her, I tried to give her money but she refused to accept my help."

Nick wondered if the Senator had kept tabs on the family through the years. "She's dead, sir, according to the daughter."

"Yes, I know. Terrible shame. Graham loved her in his own way. Probably the one actual love of his life," he speculated. "Unfortunately, he loved his wife's money more." Nick heard the Senator sigh on the other end. "Don't waste your time with Georgie. She wouldn't have sent the letters or the e-mails. She's just like her mother, proud and filled to the brim with integrity."

He'd had no personal dealings with the young woman, but nonetheless, he had kept tabs on her. After all, she was family. It wasn't her fault that her father had turned out to be so shallow.

The Senator's tone changed. "Listen, since you're down there, I was wondering if you might do me a favor and look in on a Jewel Mayfair. She runs a branch of the Hopechest Ranch. A foundation that, as you know," he added quickly, "is near and dear to Meredith's heart. My wife's afraid that Jewel might not be quite up to all the challenges running something of that nature entails. Let me give you Jewel's number," Joe offered.

"That'll make it simpler," Nick commented, flipping over a piece of paper he pilfered from the printer.

As the Senator read off the phone number, followed by the address where the foundation was located, Nick quickly wrote down everything. "Got it," he told the Senator, then added, "I'll call her later this afternoon if that's all right with you."

"Of course. No real hurry. Just keep me in the loop," the Senator requested just before he terminated the call.

Slipping the cell phone back into his pocket, he looked up and realized that his wife had been standing in the doorway to his office, listening. He smiled at the woman who had won his heart so many years ago.

"I've got him looking in on Jewel."

Meredith strode in on those long legs of hers that he had always admired. Her legs had been the first thing to catch his attention. The trim, but curvy figure—a figure she still maintained—had been a very close second. "I heard."

Joe gave her a long, knowing look. "Now maybe you can stop worrying about her."

"Maybe."

He laughed then, seeing right through her. "Your problem, Meredith, is that your heart's just too big," he told her. "You can't keep worrying about the immediate world."

"Not the immediate world," she protested, even though she had always been a soft touch. "Just the part that's related to me."

Coming up behind him, she lightly feathered her long fingers along his forearm. He wore his sleeves folded up, a symbol of his getting down to work. She'd always loved the way that looked. Loved the way he just got better looking with age, keeping his physique muscular and fit by working out and riding whenever he got the opportunity. There were telltale sprinkles of gray in his dark brown hair, but they only succeeded in making him look more distinguished.

He'd get the female vote without even trying, she thought.

Joe turned around to face her. "You know, things might be a little easier for you if you told Jewel that you're her aunt."

But Meredith shook her head, her short, golden-brown bob swaying from side to side. "That would mean that I'd have to tell her that Patsy was my sister. I've gotten Jewel to like and trust me. If she knew that I was the sister of the crazy birth mother who stabbed her father to death on the day she was born because he'd stolen Jewel and given her to a doctor who promised to place her in a good home, she might look at me differently. She certainly wouldn't trust me anymore. I can't risk that. She's been through too much already. On top of not getting any closure from Patsy because Patsy was in a mental institution when she tracked her down, don't forget Jewel also lost her fiancé and her unborn baby in that car crash they were all in. That's more than any one person should have to put up with. I just barely got her out of that depression she'd spiraled down into."

He tucked his arms around her waist. "I'd say finding out that she had such a terrific aunt might just begin to make up for the rest of it. At the very least, that should help her start to heal."

She smiled up at him, stealing a moment as she wrapped her arms about his neck. "Think you're smart, don't you 'Dr.' Colton?" she teased.

There were times he wished he was just like everyone else, that he didn't feel as if he had a mission to fulfill, a cause to champion in order to pay society back for all the good fortune he'd had during his lifetime. That if he wanted to take some time with his wife, a score of responsibilities wouldn't get in his way.

Compromising, Joe stole a quick kiss. "Yes, I do. But

only because I hung out with this really terrific, smart woman. Some of that had to rub off."

She laughed softly. "That silver tongue of yours is definitely going to get you elected." With a reluctant sigh, she disengaged her arms from around his neck. "I'd better leave you to your work."

"Promise me you'll stop worrying," he said, running his forefinger down along the furrow that had formed just above her nose, smoothing it.

"I'll try," she told him, crossing her heart. *Right after I call Clay and ask him to watch over Jewel,* she added silently. *That was what she should have done in the first place,* Meredith decided.

Joe released her just as the phone on his desk began to ring. "That's all I can ask," he told her before turning his attention to the person on the other end of the line.

Instantly, he became Senator Colton again, getting back to the ground work for his campaign.

"I've got something," Georgie announced, waving a piece of paper over her head as she walked quickly into her bedroom.

Nick was exactly where she'd left him, sitting at her computer. He tried not to type too forcefully on the keyboard because with each stroke, the card table would wobble precariously.

After a beat, he looked up from the screen on the monitor. "What?" he asked absently. Focusing, he realized that Georgie was holding one of the statements he'd printed out for her.

"I found a charge here that had to have been made in person. There's no online site for it. Baker's Jewels," she told him. When he watched her blankly, obviously waiting for more, she explained, "It's the name of a jewelry store in Esperanza."

Her one piece of good jewelry, a bracelet her mother had given her on her sixteenth birthday had come from there. She'd left that in the safety deposit box, along with the deed to the ranch and several pieces of her mother's jewelry that her mother's lover—Georgie couldn't bring herself to think of him as her father—had given her in what Georgie assumed was a moment of weakness. All the pieces of jewelry had been stolen from the safety deposit box. Something else she intended to get back along with her good name.

"I'm going there now. To the jewelry store," she added in case Nick didn't follow her. He had that faraway look in his eyes, as if pondering some deep problem. "You want to come along with me to make sure I don't make a break for it?"

She made the suggestion glibly, as if she really didn't want him along, but the truth of it was, she did. He'd awoken something within her last night, something she hadn't even realized was there. She wanted to prolong that feeling for as long as she could. Having him around did that for her.

Nick weighed his options. If he opted to go with her, it would seem as if he didn't trust her and she'd take offense. If he remained, there was a small chance she could bolt. He didn't want to be standing there with egg on his face even though the Senator had said he didn't believe she had a part in this.

Before he could say anything, his cell rang.

"Go ahead, answer it," she urged, waving her hand

at his pocket. "I've got to go round up Emmie anyway. I'll get back to you," she promised, already going out the doorway.

"Sheffield," Nick said the moment he had the phone to his ear.

"Nick, someone tried to break in last night."

He recognized the voice. Garrett Conrad, the Secret Service agent he'd left in charge while he was gone. Garrett was competent, but a little wet behind the ears.

"Garrett, I just talked to the Senator this morning. He didn't say anything about it to me."

"That's because he doesn't know yet," Garrett answered. "I wanted to tell you first and ask what you wanted me to do about it."

Damn, he was wasting his time here. He should have remained in Prosperino. "Give me the details," Nick ordered.

Garrett recited the events as he'd committed them to memory. "Whoever it was by-passed the security system somehow. Several of the surveillance cameras had black paint sprayed on their lens. The window to the downstairs library was broken. We found a gun nearby. He must have dropped it—and the credit card."

"He dropped a credit card *and* the gun?" Nick asked incredulously. Whoever had tried to break in was smart when it came to technology and seriously lacking when it came to common sense. "That's a little too pat, don't you think?"

Garrett paused, as if framing his answer. "Not every criminal belongs to MENSA."

This sounded more like the work of a high school drop-out. "What's the name on the card?"

There was noise on the other end, as if Garrett was

looking for the card. "Got it," he murmured under his breath, then read, "Georgeann Grady."

Okay, that cinched it, Nick thought. If he'd had any doubts, this erased it. Someone was definitely out to frame Georgie.

Was it a matter of someone trying to kill two birds with one stone? Or was this strictly about revenge with the focus entirely on bringing Georgie down any way they could?

"It couldn't have been her," Nick told his subordinate flatly. "Georgeann Grady has been here in Esperanza for the last two days."

"Maybe she's working with an accomplice?" Garrett suggested.

"An accomplice who is trying to implicate her?" he asked incredulously. "It doesn't make any sense. No, my guess is that someone is trying to frame her." Restless, Nick got up and began to pace. "The question is, is whoever's behind this trying to get the Senator, too, or is there some other connection we're missing?" He stopped by the window and looked out. Miles of flat land spread out before him. God, but the terrain was lonely. "Tell Steve I don't want him leaving his desk until he has a complete history on the woman. If she had so much as a schoolyard altercation in kindergarten, I want to know about it. Is that understood?"

"Understood." He could almost see Garrett snapping to attention. "I'll have him get back to you."

When he put away his phone, Nick felt the back of his neck prickling. As if he were being watched.

Glancing to the doorway, he saw Georgie. She held on to Emmie's hand. Antsy, Emmie all but danced from foot to foot.

"I had lots of 'altercations' in kindergarten," Georgie told him crisply. There wasn't even a hint of a smile on her face.

Emmie tugged harder on her hand. "What's a 'cation, Mama?"

"Altercation," Georgie corrected. "That's a fancy word for fighting."

Emmie's green eyes widened. "You punched someone out, Mama?" she asked, clearly fascinated.

Georgie wasn't ashamed of what she'd done. She'd been raised to stand up for herself. Her brothers had been proud of her. "Only when some nasty little kid called your grandmother or your mama a bad name."

"I'd altercation them too," Emmie told her solemnly, carefully enunciating the word.

It took effort not to laugh, but she didn't want to hurt her daughter's feelings. Emmie's heart was in the right place. Georgie gave her a little squeeze.

"I know you would, pumpkin. I know you would." All the while, she kept her eyes on Nick. "Why are you investigating me again?" She thought they were past this, especially after last night.

Or was she an idiot to believe that?

"Because somebody tried to make it look as if you attempted to break into the Senator's house in Prosperino. A gun and a credit card were conveniently left on the premises." He didn't want her to think he had any doubts about her innocence. "And because the laws of physics haven't been, to my knowledge, repealed in the last few days, you couldn't have been in two places at once."

"Mama rides really, really fast," Emmie offered helpfully.

Nick shook his head. "Not that fast. She would have had to have been in California and her bedroom at the same time last night."

Looking every inch like a miniature adult, Emmie nodded her head. "And she was there with you the whole time."

Startled, Nick exchanged looks with Georgie. It was Georgie who spoke first. "Emmie, how do you know where he was?"

"'Cause I went to see him in the guest room. He wasn't there. Then I went to your room and there he was. You were asleep. Was he keeping you safe, Mama?"

It was ironic that the little girl would choose those exact words.

"Yes, honey, he was keeping me safe," she told her seriously, then glanced up at Nick. "Okay, Emmie and I are off to Baker's Jewels."

He made a quick decision. "I'm coming, too," he told her.

A twinge of disappointment twisted inside of her. "Still don't trust me?"

"It's not you I don't trust," he answered, getting his suit jacket from the back of the chair and slipping it on. "I think I need to go on keeping you safe," he said, using Emmie's words. The little girl flashed him an approving grin.

His tone told Georgie that there was no way she was going to argue him out of it. She didn't bother wasting her breath.

"Okay, c'mon. Let's get going. The sooner we get to the bottom of this, the better."

"My thoughts exactly," he agreed.

Except that, she thought as she led him out of the house, once they got to the bottom of this, he'd be gone again.

She blocked out the thought as best she could. There was no point in dwelling on what she couldn't change.

Chapter 12

"Another day, another surveillance tape," Georgie quipped as they drove back from Baker's Jewels later that day.

She was referring to the surveillance tape on the seat between them. Nick had obtained it from Clyde Baker, the jewelry store owner. Clyde had come to the store to speak to them personally. Getting on in years and in progressively poorer health, he left the running of his store to his employees and his nephew, Thom.

Consequently, he had not been there on the day that "Georgie" was supposedly in to buy a very expensive diamond and ruby ring. But Thom had. However, Clyde's nephew didn't have much of a memory to draw on. To him, the woman on the surveillance tape and Georgie appeared to be one and the same, which he said as he viewed the tape.

Nick had said nothing in the store to contradict that assessment, only thanking Clyde for his cooperation and promising to return the tape "soon."

Georgie fidgeted. Nick had been quiet on the way back from town. Her exasperation got the better of her. "So now you think it's me again."

His mind elsewhere, it took him a second to focus on Georgie's accusation. He spared her a glance. "Did I say that?"

She blew out a breath, her irritation growing. "No, but you didn't *not* say that either."

"This time, two negatives don't make a positive," he told her. He'd been entertaining a new theory since they'd gotten back into the truck. At the moment, he tried to work the theory out in his head.

It took her a second to decipher his words. "So you don't think it's me." It was more of a question than a statement.

This time he looked at her for more than just a fraction of a second. "No."

She wanted more than that. She wanted something, an explanation, that would make her feel more secure. "Why not? Clyde's idiot nephew did."

Her question made him laugh softly. "You just said it yourself. His 'idiot' nephew. Obviously Thom is not a keen observer. The woman on the tape was made up to look like you, but if you watch the tape closely, you'll see the inconsistencies." The silence was pregnant. She waited for him to give an example, Nick thought. "For instance, the woman's taller than you."

"How can you tell?"

"Because on the tape, she's facing Thom over the counter and she's half a head shorter than he is. You're a whole head shorter." The corners of his mouth curved. "And you've got more curves than she does." He saw a blush rise up her cheeks and found it engagingly attractive.

"What's curves, Mama?" Emmie piped up from the confinement of her car seat in the back.

"We'll talk about that later, when you're older," Georgie promised quickly. "It'll make more sense to you then." She turned to look at Nick. "I guess this woman dressed up like me so she could get away with using my credit card."

"That's part of it," he agreed. "But I think it's more complicated than that. I think she's trying to ruin you."

Georgie snorted. That was a no-brainer, she thought. "Well, she's cleaned out my bank account and maxed out my credit cards. I'd say that she's doing more than just trying."

"Are we ruined, Mama?" Emmie asked, sounding clearly distressed.

"Not if I have anything to say about it."

Both Nick and Georgie said the same words at the same time. Hearing the other say it, they looked at one another in surprise.

Nick grinned. "Hell of an echo in here." And then he remembered Emmie was in the back, listening to everything. "Heck," he amended. "Heck of an echo in here."

Georgie laughed, appreciating the fact that Nick was trying to police his language around her daughter, although the words really had no effect on Emmie. She took solace in the fact that Nick seemed determined to come to her aid and track down this impostor. At this point, her independence didn't matter. She more than welcomed his help.

"Why would this woman be trying to ruin me?" Georgie asked.

"That's what I intend to find out," he told her. Reaching for his dark glasses, he slipped them on again. The sun seemed to bounce off everything, giving off a glare that made it hard to see. "There's an outside chance that she's got some kind of grudge against all the Coltons and you're just the first one on her hit list."

"What makes you say that?"

"Because of the e-mails to the Senator." From what he'd gathered, it had all started there. "If it was just you she was after, she would have picked someone closer to home—either that, or she would have sent threatening e-mails to the President himself. That would have gotten a really quick reaction. Instead, she picked another Colton, one who was out of state. There has to be a reason for that." He just hadn't figured it out yet, he added silently. But he would. And soon.

Georgie rolled his words over in her head. "Makes sense, I guess."

Of course, with this growing headache, it was hard to make sense of anything. Georgie absently rubbed her temples with her thumb and middle finger.

Nick caught the telltale movement out of the corner of his eye. "Headache?"

It had begun in her shoulders and moved along the circumference of her skull, from rear to front. The tension of all this had finally gotten to her.

"A big one," she acknowledged. "It's still in the forming stage."

He dug into his pocket and handed her a small bottle that contained an extra-strength, over-the-counter, pain killer. The bottle was half empty, testifying to the fact that he used the pills a great deal himself. "Here, take two of these."

"And call you in the morning?" she quipped, quoting the instructions doctors were said to give.

"Or sooner," he murmured meaningfully, unable to help himself. He kept his voice low enough for Emmie not to hear.

Georgie gave the bottle back to him, unopened. "Thanks, but I've got my own way of dealing with killer headaches. The minute we get back, I'm going out for a ride."

That would have been the *last* thing he would have done for a headache. "Won't all that jostling just make it worse?"

"Nope, clears out my head. I haven't been on a horse since I came back. Maybe I'm going through withdrawal," she kidded.

As she contemplated the ride, she began to feel better already. There was nothing like going off into the country, just her and her horse, to restore peace in her world. She'd even gone riding shortly before she gave birth to Emmie. It was in her blood. Riding for her was as natural as breathing.

Getting on the back of a horse wouldn't have been his first choice—or his twentieth—to clear his head, or any other part of him. That fact underscored that they were from two very different worlds.

He had to remember that.

"I'll only be gone for a little while," she promised Nick and her daughter, getting on the horse she'd quickly saddled.

The palomino, a three-year-old mare named Blue Belle, was the mount that she took with her when she traveled the rodeo circuit. She'd given the mare a couple of days to relax and graze, but now it was time to renew their bond and she was more than ready.

Seated in the saddle, Georgie was filled with the sense that she'd come home and that all was right with the world.

"C'mon, Belle, let's ride." It was what she said to the mare whenever they were in competition. With a toss of her head, Georgie kicked her heels into Belle's flanks and the palomino took off.

It didn't escape Nick's notice that Georgie had entrusted him with her daughter. He'd finally won her, he thought with a tinge of unexpected satisfaction.

He looked down at the little girl beside him. "Let's go inside, Emmie, and see if I can get some good shots off the tape."

The little redhead cocked her head and eyed him quizzically. "You're going to shoot it?"

Nick laughed. "No, I'm going to try to freeze the tape so that I can get a good picture of the woman who's pretending that she's your mother. Maybe someone around Esperanza will recognize her and tell me her name."

Emmie nodded. "Okay. I'll help you," she volunteered.

The little girl slipped her hand into his and then glanced over her shoulder to look at her mother one last time. It was then that Emmie froze for a second before she let out with a bloodcurdling scream. Because at that exact moment, just as Georgie, her horse going at a full gallop, was about to head for the winding path that led away from the ranch house that she suddenly slid off her mount.

The saddle came off with her and she landed on the ground, hitting her head hard.

There was less than half a second between when Nick turned to see why Emmie screamed and his breaking into a run. A sick feeling churned in his stomach.

Emmie was right beside him, pumping her small legs as quickly as she could. She had speed, he had length. They reached Georgie almost at the same time.

"Georgie!" he called even before he sank to his knees beside her.

"Mama! Mama!" Grabbing her mother's hand, Emmie shook it, trying to make her mother open her eyes.

The sick feeling inside Nick's stomach spread throughout his body. He placed his fingers against Georgie's throat. The pulse he located made his own heart leap. She was still alive.

Emmie looked at him with huge, frightened eyes. "She's not dead, right? She's not dead." It wasn't a question, it was a plea.

"No, she's not dead," he assured her, relief flooding through him.

Emmie began to cry. "Why won't she open her eyes?"

He had to calm down Emmie. The last thing he needed right now was to have a hysterical child on his hands. He wasn't equipped to handle that. "Your mother hit her head pretty hard. It knocked her out."

Emmie caught her lower lip between her teeth. It was an obvious effort to keep herself from crying. She was more adult than some adults he'd known. "Like in the cartoons?"

He had no idea what they were showing in cartoons

these days. The last cartoon he remembered was from a childhood that seemed as if it was light years away from now. He vaguely remembered that there'd been a coyote walking on thin air, falling into the chasm only when he looked down and realized that there was nothing beneath his feet.

"Not quite like in the cartoons," he told her. He rose to his feet with Georgie's unconscious body in his arms. Rather than running off, the horse she'd ridden stood like a sentry beside her mistress. He knew Georgie wouldn't want the palomino to wander off. Nick glanced at Emmie. Despite the accident, the horse seemed tame enough. "Emmie, do you think you can take the horse back to the stable?"

"Sure." The little girl obediently picked up the reins that were trailing along on the ground. Authoritatively, she said, "Let's go, Belle."

The animal trotted patiently beside her like an over-sized pet. Emmie quickly led the horse into the stable and closed the stall, then dashed across the yard to join Nick as he entered the house.

Nick placed Georgie's inert form on the sofa. Emmie dashed into the kitchen. Within a minute, she reappeared with a wet towel.

"Here," she held it out to Nick. "You put it on her head," she told him solemnly. "Mama says it makes her feel better sometimes."

"Let's hope this is one of those times," he replied as he spread the cloth on Georgie's forehead, praying that there wasn't any internal damage.

The second the cold cloth touched her skin, Georgie began to moan. And then her eyes fluttered open. They shifted from Nick to her daughter as she struggled to put her world back in order. Her head felt as if it was coming apart.

"Mama!" Emmie cried. "You're back!" Ecstatic, she threw her small arms around her mother's neck.

Nick was tempted to pull the little girl back, but he decided that both Emmie and Georgie needed this re-affirming moment. Any pain that might have been generated from Emmie's hug was more than balanced out by the warmth he knew the contact created.

"Don't cry, honey, I'm okay," Georgie comforted her daughter, slowly rubbing Emmie's back the way she used to when Emmie was a baby and needed soothing. Feeling as if she'd been trampled by a herd of horses, Georgie raised her eyes to Nick. "What happened?"

She didn't remember, Nick thought. Had there been damage? Should he be rushing her to the hospital instead of just standing here? Being grateful that she was alive? It occurred to him that he didn't even know if Esperanza *had* a hospital.

"You fell off your horse and hit your head," Nick told her.

Georgie just stared at him, certain that she couldn't have heard correctly. "No. I never fall off my horse. Not once in all those years of competition. Not since I was ten," she recalled with emphasis.

He sat down on the edge of the scarred coffee table. "You did today."

She started to shake her head, then stopped as arrows of pain shot through her. "That's not possible," she protested in a voice that was definitely having trouble remaining even.

Emmie lifted her head from Georgie's chest. "I saw you, Mama," she confirmed.

"Look, that was a pretty nasty spill. I'm going to take you to the hospital. You just wait—" Rising from the table, Nick didn't get a chance to finish.

"No, no hospital," she said, her voice growing stronger. "I don't want to go to any hospital." Georgie closed her eyes for a moment as a wave of pain washed over her. And then it began to recede. "I just want to find out what's going on here."

"You fell off your horse," Nick repeated. "The saddle came off," he elaborated. "You must have forgotten to tighten the cinch."

She gave him a look that told him she'd sooner forget to put her clothes on when she left the house than to forget to tighten her cinch. "The saddle came off?" she asked incredulously.

He nodded. "Slid right off like butter."

Upset, confused, Georgie tried to sit up and get off the sofa. The room began to spin and she lay back even before Nick gently pushed her back.

"Something's wrong," she protested. "That's a hand-tooled saddle. My grandfather gave it to my mother and she passed it on to me—"

"Then it's old," he pointed out. "Things wear out."

"Not this saddle. It's well made and it's always been lovingly taken care of. There's no reason that it should have come off Belle like that."

He knew she wasn't going to let the matter drop and he wanted her to get some rest. "I'll go check it out," he told her. He began to go, then doubled back. He didn't trust her. "But you have to promise to stay here." When she didn't say anything, he pressed the issue. "You have to promise."

Trapped, Georgie blew out a breath. Emmie had

climbed up onto the sofa and curled up on her as if she was part of the sofa. "Okay."

Nick still didn't trust her. He decided to enlist help. "Emmie, I'm making you a deputy Secret Service agent—"

"You can do that?" Emmie asked, her eyes widening again. For the first time since she'd seen her mother fall, a smile flitted along her rosebud lips.

"I can do that," he assured her. "Now, you watch your mother. And whatever you do, don't let her get up."

"Not even to go to the bathroom?" Emmie wanted to know.

"Not even then," he said, starting to leave the room.

"You're a hard man, Nick Sheffield," Georgie called after him. She winced as her voice echoed in her head.

"And don't you forget it," he tossed back over his shoulder. "I'm counting on you, Emmie," he told the little girl.

"Okay," she answered solemnly. Emmie had scrambled off the sofa and had assumed a rigid stance, carefully watching her mother for any movement.

Nick hurried outside and ran the length of the yard until he reach where the saddle was lying on the ground. About to pick it up and bring it into the house, he decided to examine it. At first glance, it appeared that Georgie was right. The saddle was in excellent condition, despite its age.

He was in foreign territory here, Nick thought, looking over the square skirt, lifting the heavily decorated fender. Unfamiliar with a saddle's construction, he had no idea what he was looking for.

And then, miraculously, he found it. Despite his ignorance, even he could identify a cut cinch when he saw one. He examined the offending length of leather. The cinch had been cut three quarters of the way through. It was torn the rest of the way.

Someone had tampered with her saddle, hoping for just this kind of a scenario. Were they out to kill her, or just to scare her? And if it was the latter, to what end?

Either way, it confirmed what he was thinking. That Georgie was the prime target. He had to make her understand that without frightening her.

Or maybe, he decided, a little fear might just do the trick. Otherwise, he had a feeling she would continue thumbing her nose and being damn reckless. It was apparently in her blood.

Georgie stared at him. What he was saying wasn't making any sense. "Cut?" He nodded. "You're sure?"

"I might not be able to lasso a steer or whatever it is you lasso around here," he told her. "But I know a cut cinch when I see one. Hey, hey, hey." She'd begun to get off the sofa again. Nick pushed her back down just as he had the first time. "Where do you think you're going?"

She didn't do helpless well. The dizziness had abated and she wanted to examine her saddle. She just couldn't believe someone would have actually done this on purpose. "I want to go see my saddle for myself."

Nick looked at her for a long moment. He'd never met someone quite like her. But right now, her stubbornness was loosing its appeal. "Why would I make that up?"

Frustration ate away at her. None of this made any sense. She felt as if she was trapped in some surreal story. "I don't know, why would you?"

"I wouldn't," he told her firmly. "Someone deliberately cut your cinch in a place you wouldn't immediately notice if you were in a hurry." And maybe there was something she hadn't realized, he thought. "If you'd fallen off your horse ten minutes later than you did, God only knows how long you would have laid there, unconscious."

No longer a sentry, Emmie was once again huddled against her, holding on as much to receive comfort as to give it. "You're scaring her," Georgie chided him.

"No need to be scared," he told her. "I'm not leaving your side until this thing gets resolved."

He had some time coming to him, time he hadn't used because there'd been no reason to use it. He wasn't the type who enjoyed flying off to some fashionably popular vacation site just to spend hours lying on a beach. He enjoyed working, being useful. Finding out who was after Georgie came under that heading.

Georgie didn't reply, but Emmie raised her head and smiled at him as if she thought he was the Angel Gabriel, sent down to protect them. It was reward enough.

Chapter 13

The silence within the house was so pervasive, it all but throbbed. Only the sound of his fingers hitting the keyboard interrupted the quiet.

Having gotten as much as he could from the computer tower in Georgie's bedroom, Nick was now working on the laptop he'd brought from Prosperino. At the moment, he used a popular software to enhance the strip of videotape he'd frozen. He attempted to isolate a decent close-up of the woman posing as Georgie in order to print a photograph. He intended to show that around town until he found someone who recognized her.

A faint noise behind him caught his attention and he was on his feet, his weapon drawn. And then he let out a breath as he saw what or rather who was responsible for the noise.

"Do you have duct tape lying around?" he asked Georgie.

She vaguely remembered seeing a round wheel of silver, but for the life of her, she couldn't recall just where. "Some place, I guess," she said with a shrug, then asked, "Why?"

"I figured I'd use it to tape you to your bed," he told her, sitting down again and turning his attention to the laptop.

He heard the smile in Georgie's voice, heard the slight rustle as she crossed to the sofa rather than back to her room as he'd hinted.

"I didn't know that Secret Service agents were allowed to be kinky."

"Nothing kinky about it," he said matter-of-factly, doing his best to concentrate. It wasn't easy with her in the room. Not when she was standing there, wearing an oversized T-shirt and what he imagined to be little else underneath. "I just want you resting."

"I'm fine," she assured him. She leaned against the sofa's overstuffed arm. "Headache's almost gone."

"If you're so fine, what are you doing up?" he asked. Rather than look at her, he glanced at his watch. "It's almost midnight."

She shrugged and the hem of her T-shirt rose dangerously high across her thighs. His thoughts went AWOL for a moment before he reined them in again. "I heard you typing."

Nick cleared his throat. It felt as dry as dust. "Sorry, I'll try to type softer."

"No, I'm sorry," she said with feeling, surprising him. "Sorry you have to put in all this extra time. Sorry you feel you need to stand guard."

In his estimation, there was no need to be sorry.

"Nothing I haven't done before." Nick assured her. And then he smiled as a distant memory floated through his mind. "This beats sitting in a car all night, making sure no one tampers with it."

"When did you do that?"

"When I first became a Secret Service agent, I got tapped to babysit the President's car the night before he flew in to tour Los Angeles," he explained. "Some sort of political fund-raiser," as he recalled. "It's kind of a rite of passage, testing the new agent to make sure he's got the stamina for boredom."

"You actually had to sit in his car all night?"

Nick nodded. "Right from the time it was certified as 'clean'—no bugs, no bombs, no surprises," he elaborated. "Everything was deemed in perfect running order. It was my job to see it stayed that way."

Georgie couldn't envision herself doing something like that. She needed to move around. "I would have gone crazy, having to sit still like that for that long," she confessed.

He'd felt the same way. "Point is," he told her, "I can stay awake for a long time and I don't mind 'guarding' you." He smiled at her, keeping his eyes on her face. "You're a lot prettier than the car was. Now go to bed." He tried to turn back to his work.

"I'm not tired," she protested. She remained leaning against the arm. "I've had too much resting as it is." Georgie decided to sit down on the sofa beside him and slid into place. She tugged the errant T-shirt down before it had a chance to ride up. "Do you mind having some company?" It was intended as a rhetorical question.

He had the uneasy feeling that one thing would lead

to another. The only way he would get anything done tonight was if she retreated and left the room.

"I'd rather you were in bed." He did his best to sound removed.

Her eyes caressed his face. "I'd rather you were there with me."

Did she have any idea how much he wanted her at this moment? He sincerely doubted it. And if he didn't get her to leave soon, he was going to act on his impulse. Still, he tried to verbally push her away by sounding flip. "I don't think you're in any shape for what that implies."

Sensing he was weakening—which was only fair because she was already there—Georgie feathered her fingertips through his hair. "You'd be surprised. I'm very resilient."

He grinned, thinking of the other night. "Not to mention incredibly flexible."

"With what I do—did," she corrected herself since rodeo competition was supposed to be in her past now, "for a living, I had to be."

He picked up on the correction. She meant to stick it out, he surmised. Good for her. "What are you going to do now?"

The future no longer looked nearly as certain as it had a little more than forty-eight hours ago. "I was going to settle down, give the rest of my life some thought. Maybe raise quarter horses." But a ranch like that required money, a good deal of it. Her voice took on a tinge of sarcasm. "But that was before my bank account suffered a crippling withdrawal—"

Nick cut in. "I'll find your money for you," he promised.

That he did so surprised him since he'd never been

one to give his word easily. He preferred coming through and having success speak for him instead of making promises ahead of time. That way, if he failed, his word wasn't compromised.

Georgie watched him for a long moment, her eyes searching his face for signs that he was just paying lip service. She didn't find any. "You're that confident?"

His mouth curved. "I'm that good."

Georgie laughed. "No shaky self-esteem problem found here."

He knew his abilities and that he usually did what he set out to do.

"Can't afford it," he said simply. "You've got to have confidence in yourself. In my line of work, you hesitate and you're not just risking your own life but the life of the person you're supposed to be guarding."

Which meant that he had to be alert twenty-four/seven. "Pretty nerve wracking way to earn a living if you ask me."

Nick inclined his head in silent agreement. "Almost as bad as galloping at break-neck speed, zigging and zagging between barrels," he commented drily.

Amused at the wording, she said, "The horse does the galloping."

He spread his hands wide, as if accepting the correction. "My mistake."

Curious, and far more relaxed than when she'd walked in, Georgie looked at what he worked on. Her mouth dropped open when she saw the blown up image he'd enhanced. Life-size, it was more startling. "My God, that almost does look like me."

"The nose is wrong," he pointed out. "Hers is sharp, yours is…perfect," he finally said for lack of a better word.

Every time she tried to shut things down inside, to

bar him access, he'd say or do some sweet little thing and throw everything off again. She might as well stop telling herself that she wasn't attracted to him because she was. And pretending that she didn't care if he stayed or left was a crock as well. She cared—even though she knew it was futile.

"You know," she told him, "for a closed-mouth person, you do say some very nice things."

He didn't quite see it that way. If anything, he was being abrupt. It was easier maintaining distance that way. "I skipped class the day they handed out silver tongues."

She thought of Jason, of how he'd gotten to her, saying things that made her lower her guard. Made her dream. "Silver tongues are highly overrated."

Nick read between the lines. "Oh? Did Emmie's father have a silver tongue?"

She stiffened and he knew he'd wandered out onto sensitive territory. But his curiosity, his need to know about her past, about the man she'd made love with, got the better of him. He told himself it was just to fill out her profile, but he knew he was lying.

Georgie sighed. Nick was going out of his way to protect her and her daughter when he clearly didn't have to. That meant she owed him. So, if he asked a question, the least she could do was answer it.

Forcing herself to relax, she said, "Yes, he did. Jason Prentiss." She gave him Emmie's father's name before Nick could ask. "I actually thought that what happened between us would last forever." God, had she ever been that naive? "Instead, it barely lasted the summer."

"Does he know?" Nick asked. When Georgie looked at him quizzically, he elaborated, "That Emmie is his?"

"He knows there's a child," she replied with a vague

shrug. "But as to sex or name, he didn't want to get 'that involved.'" She was quoting what Jason had said to her the evening she confessed that she was pregnant. "He wanted me to have an abortion. When I refused to sweep the baby out of my life, Jason quickly swept himself out of mine."

She paused for a moment before continuing. It had been a long while since she'd given Jason much thought. She'd had too much living to do to waste a moment thinking about the man she no longer loved, perhaps had never really loved.

"I don't know where he is these days and I really don't care. Looking back, he wasn't all that special." She was smarter now and could see through shallow posers like Jason. "But he did leave me with something wonderful, so I can't bring myself to hate him. Without Jason, I never would have gotten Emmie in my life." Her face was passionately animated as she said, "I can't begin to tell you what that little girl means to me."

"I think I can guess."

She grinned and laughed softly at herself. "That obvious, huh?" she asked, threading her fingers through her loose hair. As he watched, it seemed to him to shimmer like firelight.

"Only if you're conscious."

Nick studied her for a moment, thinking about the effect she'd had on him in such a very short time. He'd crossed lines because of her, stepped out of the boundaries that defined who and what he was. Moreover, he'd felt things he'd never felt before because of her. Things he didn't readily want to stop feeling anytime soon.

But he would have to, he reminded himself. Unless…

"Did you ever think about pulling up stakes, moving

away?" he asked quietly, watching Georgie's face for her reaction.

Her goal had always involved coming back here, amassing enough money to stay put and find a way to make a comfortable living in Esperanza.

"Where would I go?" She'd never even considered living anywhere else on a permanent basis. "This is home," she insisted. "I was born here. This has always been my home. This is where I belong." There'd never been any question of that in her mind. "Where would I go?" she repeated.

"Oh, I don't know." Yes he did, he knew exactly where he wanted her to go. "Washington."

"The state?" Why in heaven's name would she want to go live there? If anything, Montana or Wyoming would have been more in keeping with her way of life, not Washington.

"The city," he corrected. "D.C."

That would have been even stranger than the state. She certainly didn't belong back east. "I don't—"

He cut her off before she could say no. He wanted her to understand why he was asking. Wanted her to consider her answer before she gave it.

"If the Senator wins the election—" Nick was fairly certain that the man would win the nomination of his party "—he's going to D.C. and he'll need a protective detail with him at all times."

"And that would be you?" She already knew the answer, but hoped against hope that Nick would tell her something different. She didn't want a half a continent between them.

"I'd be one of them," he told her. He saw the look on her face and didn't have to hear what her response would be to his suggestion about moving to a large city. He already knew.

"I'm a small-town girl, Nick," she told him. "I always have been. I'd be lost in a place like Washington, D.C."

He shook his head, even as he slipped his hands about her face and then through her hair, framing her face. "Nothing small town about you, Georgeann Colton."

"Grady," she corrected softly. "I tend to think of myself as Georgie Grady. There's nothing about me that belongs to the Coltons."

He smiled and a sadness took root within him. "I tend to think of you as vibrant and exciting."

He saw laughter in her eyes and felt his pulse quicken. "That, too."

"Go back to bed, Georgie," he told her, dropping his hands. "Before I forget I'm not supposed to make love with you."

She had no desire to leave. All too soon, he'd be the one doing the leaving. She wanted to grasp as much happiness as she could in the limited amount of time she had left.

Georgie didn't get up. Instead, she feathered a kiss along his throat. "I won't break if you kiss me, Nick. I promise."

After years of holding himself in check, of controlling his every move, his resolve had frayed and reached its breaking point. He felt his pulse racing as her breath slid along his skin. "You're going to be my undoing, woman."

She laughed lightly, deliberately banishing any thoughts of all the tomorrows that loomed ahead of her. Tomorrows when this man would be gone, fulfilling his destiny and living the rest of his life without her. For now, he was here and that was all she was going to focus on. Because the rest of it was too difficult to think about.

"Everybody's got a job to do," she murmured, again, kissing his throat.

He needed no more coaxing than that. Lifting her into his arms the way he had the night before, Nick carried her to her bedroom. This time he paused not just to close the door as he had last time, but to lock it as well—just in case Emmie decided to pay her mother another unannounced nocturnal visit.

He made love with Georgie softly, gently, and for half the night, until exhaustion claimed them both and they fell asleep in each other's arms.

On his very first job, Nick had schooled himself to sleep with one eye open. Any noise that was out of place was guaranteed to wake him.

As it did this time.

Instantly alert, he sat up, listening. Someone was trying to turn the doorknob and come in. Was it Emmie? He didn't think so. She would have called out for her mother when she couldn't open the door.

Whoever was on the other side of the door released the doorknob and retreated.

Someone was in the house.

Faster than the blink of an eye, Nick was up and pulling on his pants. He zipped them up as he crossed to the door, flipping the lock he'd secured earlier. Nick yanked the door open just in time to see a shadowy figure fleeing to the living room.

Nick broke into a run.

The intruder had too much of a head start on him.

Nick barely managed to get within reaching distance. Lunging, he caught the person—a woman he now realized—by the hair.

Without a backward glance, she continued running and made it to the front door.

The forward motion when he grabbed for her hair threw him off balance because, instead of bringing the woman down, Nick found himself holding on to a wig. A red wig. It was fashioned like Georgie's hair, with a thick, long, red braid.

It was too dark for him to make out any of her features, except that she appeared to be a blonde. His gut told him that the intruder was the woman caught on the tapes from both the bank and the jewelry store.

The lights suddenly came on, robbing the shadows of their space.

But the intruder was gone.

"What's going on?" Georgie cried, her hand still on the light switch on the wall. At seeing the wig he had in his hand, a sick feeling bubbled in her stomach. She heard herself ask, "What's that?" as she nodded at his hand.

He looked at it in disgust. "I seem to have scalped your impersonator."

Georgie felt both violated and mad as hell. It was bad enough to have someone break in when she was away, but to have an intruder invade her home, her sanctuary while she was sleeping in it, made it so much worse.

"She was here?" Georgie asked hoarsely.

He nodded. "Obviously she didn't know that you'd gotten back." Georgie crossed the room and headed straight for the coffee table, where she kept one of the two phones in the house. "What are you doing?" he asked as Georgie picked up the phone receiver and began to dial.

She didn't answer until she finished dialing. It was the middle of the night, but she knew the call would automatically be transferred to Jericho Yates's home. Jericho was the county sheriff and someone she'd known for a long time.

"No offense, Nick, but I'd feel a whole lot better if we brought the sheriff in on this." She saw he was about to protest her decision, but she wasn't going to be talked out of it. She had her daughter to consider. Georgie's voice picked up speed. "You can't stay here indefinitely and watch over us and if anything happened to Emmie because of this crazy woman—"

He wanted to argue with her because he preferred to keep this contained. But his conscience wouldn't allow it. Georgie was right, he wasn't going to be here in Esperanza indefinitely. He had a life, a career, waiting for him back in California. And she would go on living here. Georgie deserved to live without fear haunting her every move.

Stepping away, he waved at the phone. "Go ahead. Tell the sheriff to come," he told her. "Just don't mention anything about the e-mails."

The phone was still ringing on the other end. She covered the mouthpiece. "Why not?"

"Because that falls under my jurisdiction," he reminded her.

She didn't see how he could separate one issue from the other, but she didn't protest. She just wanted this impostor, this creature who'd taken her money, her name, her life, caught and punished.

A deep, sleepy voice came on on the other end. "Yates."

"Sheriff, this is Georgie Grady. Someone just tried to break into my house. Could you please come by first thing in the morning?"

"I'll do better than that, Georgie," the sheriff told her. "I'll be there in half an hour."

Chapter 14

True to his word, Sheriff Jericho Yates was standing in her doorway within twenty minutes.

Georgie had had only enough time to throw on clothes. Nick had gotten dressed and then done something on his computer that she hadn't had time to look at yet, but Nick had looked pleased with the outcome. He was in the process of printing whatever it was he'd come up with when the Sheriff had rung her doorbell. She'd flown to answer it.

Georgie didn't recognize the man standing next to the sheriff. The latter wore the uniform of a deputy and was a little shorter than Jericho. But then, at six feet three inches most people were a little shorter than Jericho. And, she'd come to know, a hell of a lot more cheerful than the serious thirty-five-year-old.

Tall, broad-shouldered and lean-hipped, Jericho

Yates was a wall of solid muscle. Wearing his dark blond hair long and some facial stubble, he looked more like Hollywood's version of an old-fashioned lawman out of the 1800s. But the thing about Jericho was that, despite the fact that he hardly ever smiled and never used twenty words when three would do, he inspired confidence in the people he dealt with and protected. People felt safe when he was around, even though his territory stretched out beyond Esperanza to include the entire county.

Jericho's hazel eyes swept over her as he nodded a greeting. When his eyes shifted to look at Nick, they hardened just a touch. Strangers were subjected to close scrutiny.

Now, with the house lit up and the sheriff and his deputy, not to mention Nick all standing around her, Georgie felt a little foolish about the momentary attack of anxiety that had caused her to call the sheriff.

"I really didn't mean for you to come out to the ranch in the middle of the night, Sheriff."

Jericho's expression never changed, but she had the definite impression that he was looking right into her head.

"You wouldn't have called if you didn't. You would have waited until morning." Again, his eyes shifted over toward Nick.

The Secret Service agent had never felt himself being dissected and measured so quickly before, even when he'd originally applied for his present position. Leaning forward, one hand on Georgie's shoulder in an un-spoken gesture signifying protection, he extended his hand to the sheriff. "I'm Nick Sheffield."

The deputy, who clearly was trying to emulate his boss, asked, "You a friend of hers, Nick Sheffield?"

"In a manner of speaking," Nick said, busy with his own process of measuring and dissecting. The sheriff was coming from a position of confident strength. He got the impression that the deputy had yet to achieve that for himself.

She felt tension in the air, or maybe that was just her. Clearing her throat, Georgie decided to get the introductions out of the way.

"Nick, this is Sheriff Jericho Yates. And—" Her voice trailed off as she realized something. "I'm sorry," she told the deputy, "I don't know who you are."

Maybe it was her, but she felt like there'd been an influx of a great many new faces in Esperanza since she'd left. The town was clearly growing. Until this moment, she hadn't realized how much she liked being able to recognize everyone she passed on the street until that ability was lost to her.

Jericho came to her rescue. "This is my new deputy, Adam Rawlings." He was still breaking in the man, but all things considered, Rawlings was coming along nicely. The deputy, he noted out of the corner of his eye, flashed a guileless smile at Georgie and then her "friend." "Anything missing?" Jericho asked as he walked into the house. He scanned the area and it didn't look as if anything had been disturbed.

This most recent break-in was the legendary straw that had broken the camel's back. Words just came pouring out. "The money out of my bank account. My mother's jewelry. My—"

Jericho stopped her, appearing slightly puzzled as he tried to make sense out of what she'd just said. "You emptied your bank account and then brought the money home?"

Frustrated, Georgie backtracked. "No, *she* emptied my bank account—*and* my safety deposit box and she was probably the one who's responsible for maxing out all of my credit cards."

Jericho held his hand up. "Slow down, Georgie," he instructed. When she stopped talking, he asked, "'She?'"

Georgie's head bobbed up and down. "The woman who's passing herself off as me. Right down to the wig." The second she mentioned the wig, she moved over to the coffee table where Nick had deposited the disguise. She held it up for the sheriff to see.

"She broke into the house at about three-thirty," Nick estimated. "I woke up when I heard her trying the doorknob—"

"To the house?" Jericho asked.

"No, to the bedroom. The door was locked." Jericho said nothing, but his silence spoke volumes. "I tried to get her but she had too much of a head start on me. She escaped."

"But one of you managed to scalp her," Adam added wryly, humor twisting his mouth. Jericho shot him a reproving look before turning his attention back to Nick.

He nodded toward the wig. "We're going to have to take that in as evidence."

Nick would have been disappointed if the man hadn't suggested that.

"You might want to run it for DNA," he encouraged. The Sheriff merely looked at him as if he'd suggested taking the wig dancing. "One of her own hairs might have gotten stuck in the wig."

"Watch a lot of TV, do you?" There wasn't even a single hint of amusement in the sheriff's voice.

"I was a cop in L.A.," Nick countered. They didn't

have the finest lab in the country, but at least they had access to it.

"That would explain it," Jericho murmured under his breath. "We don't have a forensic lab here. That'll have to go to San Antonio for processing. Might be six months before we hear anything. Maybe more. In the meantime—" he turned toward Georgie "—you know anyone who would want to do you harm?"

"Not off the circuit. And not really on either," she amended quickly. "Just knocked out of the running. But I've given up rodeoing." There, she'd said it out loud and made it public with someone who was in contact with most of Esperanza. The sheriff wasn't a talker, but word would get around. Not like lightning, more like the widening ripples in the lake after a rock was tossed in. "It's time I settled down. Emmie's going to be in kindergarten in the fall."

Jericho nodded. "Got a plastic bag we could use?" he wanted to know, then nodded toward the evidence that was back on the coffee table. "For the wig."

"Sure. I'll go get it." Georgie turned on her heel and went to the kitchen to find a plastic bag for the sheriff. So far, she was lucking out. Emmie was still asleep, but that was subject to change and she wanted these official-looking men out of her house before the little girl was up.

Nick stepped forward. He took the photograph he'd just printed out before Jericho and his man had arrived. He handed it over to the sheriff now. "You might want to pass around this photograph, see if anyone knows her."

Jericho took the snapshot from him and examined it for a long moment. It was of a young blond woman. "You had time to take her picture?"

"That's off a surveillance tape. She was using one of Georgie's credit cards to buy herself a diamond ring. When I pulled off her wig just now, I saw she had blond hair, so I changed the clip around, gave her blond hair," Nick told him.

Jericho studied the photograph, then raised his eyes to Nick's face. He had as many questions about him as he had about the woman in the photo. "Who the hell did you say you were?"

They both knew he hadn't identified himself beyond his name. "Just a concerned friend who wants to see Georgie reunited with her money."

"Right."

It was obvious by his tone that Jericho didn't believe him for a second, but for the time being, his skepticism didn't matter. They had to find this woman.

"Mind if I take a look, Sheriff?" Adam asked, nodding at the photograph.

"Help yourself." Jericho handed over the photograph, then waited for some kind of comment. "Recognize her?" he prodded.

Wide shoulders rose up and down in a noncommittal shrug. He had the photograph back to the sheriff. "Looks a lot like Miss Grady."

"That's the whole point," Jericho told his deputy patiently.

"Yeah, I guess it is," Adam agreed sheepishly.

It struck Nick that as far as deputies went, this one wasn't the sharpest knife in the drawer.

Georgie returned with a plastic bag. It still had the faint smell of the apples she'd just emptied out about it. Jericho nodded at her, then deposited the wig inside the bag, tucking in the long braid. It was a tight fit.

Jericho paused to ask her a few more questions, then seemed satisfied for the time being.

"We'll be back," he promised her, slipping the photograph that Nick had created into the front pocket of his shirt.

Georgie walked the two men to the door. "Thank you for coming so fast."

Opening the door, Jericho paused one last time. He glanced at his deputy. "I could leave Rawlings here to watch the house," he offered.

"That won't be necessary," she assured the sheriff quickly. She glanced over at the man who had shared her bed. "I've got Nick."

Again, there was no indication what he thought of her answer. "And that worked out pretty good for you, didn't it?" He was clearly referring to the fact that the intruder had broken in and gotten as far as she had with this "Nick" in attendance.

A wave of defensiveness rose within her. Her green eyes slanted toward Nick. "Overall, yes," she informed the sheriff quietly.

"Suit yourself," Jericho told her. "I'll be in touch," he repeated, tipping his hat to her, then nodding at Nick.

"Want some coffee?" she asked as soon as she had closed the door and the sheriff and deputy were on their way.

Nick glanced at his watch. It was barely five o'clock. "Why don't you go back to bed?" he suggested gently.

Georgie shook her head. There was no way she could go back to sleep.

"Too keyed up. Dawn's almost here anyway." She sighed. How had everything fallen apart like this? *Was* there someone out to get her? The very thought was guaranteed to keep her awake nights. "Might as well get ready for it."

Being with her this short time had made him a student of the inflections in her voice. He recognized that tone. She was too anxious to sleep.

"Then I'll take that coffee," he told her, following her into the kitchen. "As long as you hold back on the asphalt."

She laughed. "I'll see what I can do."

He couldn't talk Georgie out of coming with him, although God knew he'd tried. Knowing that the sheriff could only devote a small amount of time to finding the woman in the photograph, he'd printed up more than a hundred and got to work questioning people.

It was a day later and his showing the photograph around to the various shops, restaurants and bars in Esperanza had finally paid off.

The affable bartender/owner at Joe's Bar & Grill recognized the blonde.

He rubbed a cloth over the permanently scarred and stained counter as if it was second nature to him. "That looks just like the little girl who came to me looking for a job a while ago." He took a second look in the sparse light. It was the middle of the day outside, but inside the bar it was on the cusp of midnight. "I didn't have an opening, but I had her fill out an application anyway, in case one came up."

"You still have that application?" Nick had asked.

"Well, sure. Somewhere." The answer was meant to end the conversation, not tear it wide open.

"Would you mind getting it?" Nick asked. When the bartender remained where he was, massaging the counter, Nick took out a fifty and placed it in the path of the man's towel. He stopped rubbing.

Favoring his left foot, the bartender lumbered into the back to an overcrowded, small storage room. Nick followed with Georgie shadowing his every step. He would have felt a great deal better leaving her home but Georgie refused to be left.

It took the bartender a few minutes and several curses before he came across the application. The paper was stuck in a manila folder that had an altercation with a bottle of beer. Consequently, some of the writing was gone. But just enough still visible for Nick to piece together an address. He hurriedly wrote it down on the pad he carried with him.

"Okay," Georgie declared the second he handed the folder back to the bartender, "what are we waiting for? Let's go."

"I'll take you home," he told her.

"You will not," she informed him in no uncertain terms. "Whose life did she steal? Whose house was she squatting in?" Georgie demanded as they walked back out into the sunlight. "Mine, not yours. Mine," she repeated. "There's no way you're going to confront this Rebecca Totten without me," she told him.

He had a feeling that she meant that. That even if he brought her home, she'd follow him. She got a good look at the address as well. And because they'd left Emmie with Clay early this morning, there was no stopping Georgie from doing just that.

He could stand here and argue with her, but that would waste time. She was more stubborn than a legendary mule, even if she was a hell of a lot prettier.

"If you think that I'm going to let you—"

Nick threw up his hands, not wanting to listen to any more of her tirade. "Okay," he declared, knowing he was going to regret this, "You can come."

"Damn straight I can come," she shot back, striding to where they had parked his car. "Woman steals my money, taking food out of my child's mouth, not to mention my good name, there's no way I'm not going to take care of business," she informed him hotly. Reaching the vehicle, she waited for him to unlock the door.

Nick hit the proper button on his key ring. The car made a piercing noise and all four of the locks popped open.

"You know, you can put it down," Nick told her just as she got in on the passenger side.

"Put what down?" she asked, confused.

He rounded the trunk and then got in on the driver's side, slamming the door a little louder than he'd intended. "That chip on your shoulder."

"Just drive," she told him.

He backed out of the space, then put his car in gear. They drove down the main thoroughfare. "We don't know if this Rebecca is really the one we're looking for," he pointed out.

Rebecca was the one. She could *feel* it in her bones. But to forestall another argument, she told him, "Don't worry, Nick, I promise I won't punch her out until we have proof."

"Why doesn't that comfort me?" Nick shook his head as he took a right turn on the next corner. Georgie Grady was one of a kind, all right.

There was no answer when he knocked. After a second time, he took out his cell phone.

"Who are you calling?" she asked.

"A friend of mine to see if we can get a search warrant."

"That's going to take time," she complained.

"Yes, it is. You have any better ideas?" It was a rhetorical question. He didn't expect an answer. Waiting for his friend to pick up the phone on the other end of the line, Nick turned around to look at Georgie.

"Oh, look, she left the door open," Georgie announced glibly, turning the knob and walking in.

The door had been locked less than two minutes ago. An answering machine kicked in on the other end of his call. Nick cut it off, shutting the phone. "How did you learn to do that?" he asked.

"A girl picks things up along the way" was all she said. He had no need to know that Ryder had taught her how to pick a lock, or that Ryder was currently serving time in prison.

Once inside the small apartment, Nick pulled on a pair of rubber gloves before he started to methodically go through Rebecca Totten's things.

Impressed by the gloves, Georgie smiled. "You certainly come prepared," she commented.

"Saves time," was all he said.

Since she didn't want to leave any incriminating fingerprints here herself, Georgie put on a pair of work gloves she had stuffed into her back pocket and undertook her own search.

Because of the size of the apartment—little more than a studio—the search went quickly. There was nothing hidden in the bureau drawers, or, it appeared, the closet. Nothing in the tiny pantry either.

But the apartment came with a Murphy bed and when he pulled it down, Nick hit the jackpot. The unimaginative woman had succumbed to a cliché and hidden incriminating evidence under her mattress.

"Well, she's obviously not a professional," he murmured, letting the bed, now unmade, pop back up into the wall. He held the folder he'd extricated.

Georgie, on her knees examining the contents of pots that were stacked inside the stove, looked up excitedly. "You found something?"

The question wasn't even out of her mouth before she hurried over to join him in the tiny area designated as the "bedroom."

The folder contained several photographs of Georgie and a couple of the Senator. There were also a few receipts stuffed into the folder, including one for the wig *and* one for the ring from the jewelry store that had captured her on tape.

Nick almost found it amusing. What did the woman intend to do, use the receipts for tax purposes when she filed her 1040? Would she identify them as items bought in order to commit identity theft?

Or were the receipts intended for someone else to act as proof of what she was doing?

"We got her, don't we?" Georgie asked excitedly, clutching the large book she'd been going through in hopes of shaking loose evidence that might have been stored inside.

"Looks like," he agreed. "Right down to her crooked little feet."

Georgie closed her eyes, exhaling a deep sigh of relief. She tucked the folder into an oversized book that was on the coffee table in order to keep the photographs from bending. "Oh, God, it's over. The nightmare's really over."

That was when she heard it.

The sound of a gun being cocked.

Georgie turned around slowly to find herself looking at a young, petite blond woman who looked like her only in so far as they were both roughly the same age and had the same complexion.

"Not yet," Rebecca Totten told her. She held a gun directly at them. "You know, if you two stand just like that, one in front of the other, I can kill both of you using just one bullet. I like being frugal," she said, an unnerving smile curving her mouth. And then she sighed. "I really wasn't counting on this. You weren't supposed to figure out who I was," she said, seeming clearly put out. "But then, that's what makes life interesting, isn't it? All the twists and turns that you can't predict."

She looked at Georgie, her quirky smile deepening. "Bet you never predicted it would end like this. And, for what it's worth, I am sorry. But you are going to have to die. You know that, right?"

Even as she asked the question, the blonde raised her hand and took careful aim. Her hand began to tremble. Uttering a curse, she took hold of her right hand with her left, intending to steady it so that her aim was true.

Chapter 15

The moment she saw the gun, adrenaline surged through Georgie at the speed of light. Operating purely on instinct, she launched the book she held at Rebecca's arm to deflect the shot.

At the same moment, Nick threw his body in front of Georgie to keep her from being hit by the bullet. Seeing the book hit the woman, he dived for Rebecca, bringing her down. Grabbing her right arm, he forced it up so that the gun barrel was aimed at the ceiling as he tried to disarm her.

"No, no," the blonde cried wildly, frightened as she struggled for possession of the weapon.

Georgie scrambled to her feet, searching for something to use as a weapon or to knock Rebecca out. There was nothing readily available.

The sound registered belatedly.

A single, deafening shot going off.

For a split second, Georgie froze. She'd been around the sound of guns all her life, but this time, it was surreal.

A sick feeling twisted the pit of her stomach as she swung back around. Nick was on the floor, on his knees. There was blood all over him.

"Nick!" she screamed, fear all but gutting her.

Darkness swirled around her, threatening to swallow her whole. She fought to keep it at bay. It took a long, life-draining moment before she realized that Nick hadn't been hurt. That the blood that covered his signature black suit wasn't his, but belonged to the woman he now held in his arms.

"I'm all right. Call for an ambulance," he ordered Georgie. And then he looked at Rebecca. He could all but see the life force ebbing away from her. The woman was dying. He needed to know the answer before she was gone. "Rebecca, did someone put you up to this?"

The blonde's eyes were unfocused, staring off at something that was beyond his shoulder. Fear and bewilderment etched themselves into her pale, young features.

"It…wasn't…supposed to be…like…this…"

They were the last words she uttered.

Watching, holding her breath, Georgie squeezed the cell phone in her hand. "Is she…?"

The word didn't need to be said out loud. Nick nodded, then gently slipped his hand over Rebecca's eyes, closing them. Very carefully, he lowered the body onto the floor and then got up. Everything else was left just as it was, including the gun they had wrestled over, the gun that had been twisted so that it fired into her chest instead of his.

He'd literally dodged a bullet that time, he thought cynically, relieved to still be standing.

"You're not hurt, are you?" she cried. Not waiting for an answer, she pulled back the sides of his suit jacket, anxiously looking for holes.

He'd seen enough death to be rendered numb to it, but this one had shaken him. The young woman's life force had all but slipped through his fingers.

Glancing down at himself, he looked for a telltale hole that might have been the source of at least part of the blood flow. He knew that some victims of gunshot wounds didn't even feel the bullet entering and his entire body had numbed and tensed.

But there was no hole, no wound. All the blood belonged to Rebecca.

"No," he murmured almost distantly. "But this is going to generate one hell of a cleaning bill."

"Shut up," Georgie cried, throwing her arms around him and just holding him, grateful beyond words that he was still alive.

Nick looked over Georgie's shoulder at the body on the floor.

What a waste, he thought. What a useless waste. Rebecca Totten looked to be in her twenties, if that old. Ten minutes ago, she had her whole life ahead of her, and now, now there was nothing.

Very gently, he extricated himself from Georgie's hold. "Call the sheriff, Georgie," he instructed woodenly.

Stepping back, still holding the cell phone in her hand, Georgie did as she was told. Less than a minute later, the other end was being picked up. "Yates," a deep voice announced.

Her pulse still pounding, not to mention her head, Georgie drew in a long cleansing breath, then began talking.

Jericho and his deputy had been less than a mile away when the call came in. They were there, at the studio apartment, in under five minutes. The sheriff quickly took in the scene, his hazel eyes sweeping from one end of the studio apartment to the other, coming to rest on the woman on the floor.

"Dead?" he asked Nick. The latter nodded. Jericho squatted over the body without touching her, slowly absorbing everything. "How did she happen to get that way?" His even, low tone gave no clue as to what he was thinking.

"Self-defense," Nick replied.

Jericho rose, shifting his penetrating look to the Secret Service Agent. "We'll get back to that," he promised mildly. "Secure the scene, Rawlings," he told his deputy.

"Yes, sir," Adam murmured.

A thorough search of the small studio apartment yielded the final damning evidence. Under a pile of clothes in the back of the walk-in closet was an old gym bag. It was crammed full of money. Nearly three hundred thousand dollars.

Georgie's money.

Nick took a quick inventory of the amount after Jericho handed it over to him. "Looks like you're going to be getting that horse ranch after all," Nick commented.

"That's evidence for now," Jericho warned. "But there's no reason it won't be available to you soon," he added, his voice softening slightly.

The elation Georgie felt at actually recovering her life's savings was tempered in the next heartbeat by not just the pall of death, but the haunting realization that Nick would be leaving. The threat against the Senator was over.

She couldn't bear the idea of there being half a continent between them, be it California or Washington, D.C., and yet, pride kept her from asking him to stay. Especially because she wasn't sure of his answer. He'd seemed too focused on advancing his career when they talked last night.

And if she asked him to stay and he said no, it would drive a stake through her heart.

"Call the doc," Jericho said to his deputy. "Tell him we have a body for him." It was far from a usual occurrence. When Rawlings made no move to comply, Jericho paused to glare at him. The deputy looked pale. "You all right, Adam?"

Adam blew out a breath. Unable to draw his eyes away from the prone body when he first walked in, now he avoided looking at the dead woman.

"No," Rawlings said in a low voice. And then, because the single word begged for a follow-up, he explained, "I've never seen a dead body before."

Jericho nodded, understanding. "Not exactly a common sight around Esperanza. At least, not like that. Folks around here tend to die of natural causes, not from lead poisoning." Rawlings went to summon the doctor the department had on retainer. Jericho turned his attention to Nick and the next step in procedure. "I'm going to need a statement." Jericho's words took in Georgie as well. "From both of you.

"No problem," Nick replied. He wasn't aware that

he slipped his arm protectively around Georgie, but Jericho was. He noted, too, that she made no effort to shrug the arm away.

It was another two hours before Nick and Georgie were finally back in his car, driving to her ranch. But first they needed to stop by her brother's place to pick up her daughter.

The air was pregnant with the smell of impending rain. The silence between them grew oppressive.

Nick broke the silence first.

"Come with me," he said without any preamble. He spared her a glance before turning back to the monotonous road that stretched out before him. "Pack your things, pack up Emmie and come with me." The two sentences probably qualified as the most impulsive thing he'd ever said.

She could feel her heart aching already. But this wasn't just about her, or even just about them. There was Emmie to think of. Emmie, who deserved the best she could give her. Emmie, who deserved the chances she never had. "I can't."

"Why not?" Even as he formed the question, he knew the answer. But if he talked fast enough, maybe it wouldn't come. "By your own admission, you've been going from place to place at a moment's notice. Here today, someplace else tomorrow, living inside a rattling tin can on wheels." He looked at her again. God help him, he didn't want to stop looking at her. Ever. She was like a fever in his blood. He struggled to be rational. "I can offer you something a lot better than that."

Georgie clenched her hands in her lap, as if that could

somehow ground her. "I know, and I'm tempted. Oh, God, Nick, you have no idea how much I'm tempted—"

If she felt that way, what was the problem? "Then come."

"I can't," she repeated, her voice threatening to break.

He could feel his patience unraveling. It seemed so damn simple from the outside. *Could* be so damn simple. "For God's sake, why not?"

How did she make him understand when even her own heart was rebelling against her? "Because ever since I had Emmie, this was the plan. To make enough money to finally give her a home, something secure. Something my brothers and I didn't have, no matter how hard my mother tried. Money buys you security."

His hands tightened on the wheel as he struggled to understand and to be gracious. "So if I hadn't found that gym bag in the back of Rebecca's closet, I would have had a better chance of your coming with me."

She still wouldn't have left. Because this was Emmie's home. This were where their roots were and roots were oh so important to both of them.

"Don't," she begged. "Please don't." She blinked back tears. "You could stay here."

He saw no prospects for work in a place like Esperanza. "And do what?"

"Love me."

He felt his heart twist in his chest. "Not that that isn't a tempting proposition, but I need to be able to provide for you," he pointed out.

"No, you don't," she protested quickly. "I've got enough money to last us for a while. And then there's the ranch."

He wasn't cowboy material and they both knew it.

And no way would he live off her earnings. "That's not how it works," he told her.

A ragged sigh escaped her lips. Turning her head so that he wouldn't see her tears, Georgie looked out the side window. "I know."

The first thing Nick did when he arrived back in California was report to the Senator, who was still at his Prosperino estate. He found the man in his den, going over the latest draft to his next speech.

Joe Colton seemed delighted to see his chief Secret Service agent back.

Nick closed the door behind him. "It's over, sir."

Joe immediately thought of the threatening e-mails. The flow, according to his people, had ceased just before Nick had left for Texas. "You caught the man?"

"Woman," Nick corrected. "Turned out to be a twenty-one-year-old ex-waitress from Reno. Rebecca Totten."

The name meant nothing to the Senator. "Tell me, did she say what she had against me?"

Nick shook his head. "She didn't say much of anything."

Very quickly, Nick ran through the events, giving the Senator as succinct a version of the last five days as he could. He left out certain details, all of which had to do with Georgie. In his opinion, they neither added nor subtracted from the narrative.

Joe looked pleased at how things had been resolved, although he made it clear that he regretted that the young woman paid for her misdeeds with her life.

"Great job, Nick. I really appreciate your going the extra mile on this. Or extra several thousand miles as the case may be." Joe flashed the smile he was so famous for, the one that was from the heart and guileless and had won him such a huge following. He settled back in his chair. "Tell me, how's my niece doing?" he asked, noting that any reference to her was conspicuously missing.

Nick's voice was clipped as he said, "I managed to recover her money, so she can get on with her life, setting up a ranch to breed quarter horses."

Joe's smile widened. "From what I hear, that sort of thing is in her blood. Her older brother, Clay, has a ranch around there, too."

"I met him," Nick volunteered cautiously, wondering if this was going somewhere or if it was just harmless conversation.

Joe nodded. From where he stood, the head of his Secret Service detail seemed preoccupied. "Something wrong, Nick?"

"Jet lag," Nick told him a little too quickly.

"Uh-huh." Joe eyed him knowingly—or was that just his imagination? Nick wondered. "Why don't you take some time off to deal with that?" the Senator suggested. "You've more than earned it."

Time off was the *last* thing he needed. He needed to fill up his days with routines, not have them empty so that he could spend his time thinking.

"If it's all the same to you, sir," Nick said, "I'd rather just get right back into it. I've been away from the job too long."

Joe laughed, shaking his head. "Seems to me, you've been on it all this time."

Nick shrugged. "It's what I'm paid to do," he replied. "If there's nothing else—"

"Not right now," Joe answered.

With a nod, Nick took his leave. The moment he walked away from the Senator's den, he threw himself into his work. The first order of business was to get a complete update from the agent he'd left in charge about what had been going on in his absence.

And all the while, as he worked, reviewing schedules, planning for contingencies, Nick struggled to block out any and all extraneous thoughts. Extraneous thoughts that involved a woman with flaming red hair and eyes the color of a field of four-leaf clovers.

It was a losing battle.

Nick knew when he was licked. After two days of trying to get the upper hand and place his life back on the course it had been on these last few years, he was forced, for his own sanity, to surrender.

The first step was to tell the Senator that he needed to resign.

"Do you mind if I come in?" he asked the Senator, popping his head into Joe's office.

In the midst of packing up for yet another fund-raiser, this one taking place in Phoenix the next afternoon, Joe stopped what he was doing and beckoned Nick into his study.

"Come on in," he urged. Noting the serious expression on the Secret Service agent's face, Joe wondered if any more e-mails had surfaced. "What's on your mind?"

Tip-toeing around a subject had never been Nick's way. "Your niece, sir."

For a split second, Joe looked mildly surprised. And then he smiled. "Took you a while, didn't it?"

He'd thought he'd hidden his feelings rather well.

The Senator's question caught him off guard. "Excuse me, Senator?"

Joe laughed. "Don't play dumb with me, Nick. It doesn't suit you." Pausing to pour two fingers of Napoleon brandy for both himself and his, he felt, about-to-be-ex-head of Secret Service, Joe held out one glass to Nick. "I could see it when you came back to report to me."

Accepting the glass, Nick looked at him, puzzled. "See what?"

"That you didn't belong here anymore," Joe answered simply. "You belong back there, with her."

Nick paused to take a sip. The amber liquid warmed a path down to his gut. "I don't think I 'belong' anywhere," he confessed. "Esperanza is a one-horse town."

"It's a little bigger than that," Joe assured him. He'd kept tabs on its progress, as he did on everything that interested him. "And it's growing all the time. Man of your capabilities and talents can find a lot of opportunities there—or make your own. Heading a security firm comes to mind," he commented just before he took a sip of the brandy himself. "Seems to me that you've already found the most important thing."

He'd always admired and respected the Senator and enjoyed being privy to the man's insight whenever he could. He was going to miss that, he thought. "What's that?"

"The love of a good woman."

Joe looked at the framed photograph that stood on his desk. It was of Meredith and him taken on one of their all-too-brief vacations. He couldn't recall the location, only that something had caught her fancy and she'd been laughing when her image was captured, forever freezing the moment. Looking at the photograph now, he could almost hear her laughter. Warm like sunshine, he thought.

"Trust me, Nick, everything else is a distant second." Placing his glass of brandy on his desk, Joe put out his hand. "Much as I hate to lose you—and I do—this is the best reason in the world for you to leave."

"I'll stay until my replacement's trained," Nick promised, but Joe shook his head.

"Don't even give it another thought. Just go, get the girl," Joe encouraged.

"All right, then," Nick said, more than ready to do just that. "I need to ask a favor, sir."

Joe smiled at him warmly. "If it's in my power, it's yours."

Georgie couldn't sleep. Sighing, she surrendered to the haunting insomnia. That made two nights in a row now that she'd tossed and turned, exhausted and too keyed up to sleep.

By all rights, she thought angrily, she should be sleeping like a baby. Her name had been cleared, her money and her jewelry had been restored. Even the credit card companies had been convinced to cover their losses, restoring her credit along with her good credit standing. All of that had been Nick's doing and it meant that she could get on with her life unimpeded.

But despite all that, her life felt as if it was stuck in a tar pit and she couldn't move forward. Couldn't move because her heart was no longer a functioning part of her anatomy. It was two or three thousand miles away.

Where the hell was Prosperino, California, anyway? she wondered impatiently.

A sound she couldn't quite identify nudged its way into her consciousness.

What *was* that? Thunder?

No, this was constant, she realized, sitting up. Thunder rolled and then lightning flashed. This just continued. Besides, the weather forecast called for clear skies for the next day or so.

The only place it was raining was in her heart, she thought.

The unidentified noise sounded as if it was getting closer.

Georgie kicked off the sheet she'd had covering her. Leaving the shelter of her bed, she grabbed her robe and went to the front door. Might as well satisfy her curiosity if she couldn't satisfy anything else.

Her hand was on the doorknob, about to open the door in order to see what she could see. The knock startled her, causing a stifled gasp to escape.

Who the hell would be out this early, paying her a call? There was a chain on her door, fallout from her experience with that woman posing as her. She left it in place and cautiously opened the door a crack.

Her mouth dropped open. Fumbling with the chain, she yanked the door open.

"Nick?"

He smiled at her sheepishly. "It's me," he confirmed. The last word was muffled as Georgie framed his face with her hands and kissed him hard and long.

If this was a dream, she wanted to get the most out of it before it faded, she thought, her head spinning.

But it didn't fade.

And from her experience, dreams did *not* kiss like that.

Breathless, she dropped her hands to her sides and

took a step back, still half expecting him to vanish. After two sleepless nights, she was a perfect candidate for hallucinations.

He was still here, clutching flowers whose heads were bent.

"What are you doing here?" she cried, squeezing the question out.

"I came back," was his simple reply. And then he added, "To give you these." He thrust the bouquet of slightly wilting daisies into her hands. It was a pathetic offering, but when a man proposed and had no ring, he needed to bring something. Flowers were all he could think of and she'd mentioned liking daisies. "I had the pilot set the helicopter down in a field so I could pick them for you." He shrugged, embarrassed at the offering. "It was all I could find. They don't have twenty-four-hour flower shops."

She grinned, blinking back tears. He was here, he was really here. It didn't matter for how long, what mattered was that he was here. She pressed her lips together, feeling positively giddy, her thoughts making no sense. That was the only explanation for her saying, "Maybe you could open one."

"Mama?"

The sleepy voice belonged to Emmie who was standing in the living room, rubbing her eyes. When she focused them, the grin that came over her face threatened to split it in two.

"Nick!" she cried happily. The next moment, she broke into a run and launched herself into his arms.

Dropping to his knees, he scooped her up, love, unbidden, flooding through his veins.

"Mr. Sheffield," Georgie corrected her daughter, sniffing to keep the tears back.

"How about Daddy?" Nick suggested.

Stunned, Georgie looked at him. She *was* hallucinating, she thought. She had to be. But still the mirage remained where it was.

"What?"

"These are for you," he was saying to Emmie, taking out a very small, kid-sized pair of handcuffs. He'd obtained a pair and meant to mail them to her. Bringing them in person seemed like a better idea. "I got a junior set just for you."

But Georgie was still stuck on his last statement. "Nick, what are you saying?" Georgie demanded. "Why are you telling her to call you Daddy?"

"Because I want you—both of you," he clarified, looking at Emmie first, then Georgie, "to marry me."

"Yes!" Emmie cried before her mother could say anything, tightening her hold around his neck.

Georgie looked at him, dazed. She'd had time to think. Time to regret. As much as she felt her life was here, life without Nick was barren. The first two days had hardly moved. She had no reason to believe the days after would be any better.

"Do you really mean it?" she asked him, stunned and overjoyed at the same time.

"If I don't, that helicopter pilot who flew me here is going to be really ticked off. He wanted to take off at dawn, not in the middle of the night." But once the Senator had made the proper calls to facilitate the trip, Nick had been too eager to wait a minute longer.

Georgie pressed her lips together, her head whirling as she tried to make plans. "It's going to take me a little while to settle up," she calculated, "put the ranch up for sale—"

Nick interrupted her. "But then where will we live?" he wanted to know. "More important, where would the horses live?"

Georgie came to a screeching halt, completely confused. What was he saying to her? "What?"

Nick grinned, spelling it out for her. "I'm staying here. With you. God knows there's got to be something I can do besides shield people with my body."

She remembered he'd done just that in Rebecca's apartment. This time, Georgie didn't bother wiping away her tears. She kissed this man who had captured her heart long and hard, with all her soul. "Don't be too hasty, I like being shielded."

"Then it's yes?" he asked, not bothering to hide how important her answer was to him.

"Say yes, Mama," Emmie urged. "Say yes!"

"Yes," Georgie declared, laughing and crying at the same time. And then she regained a little control over herself. "I love you, Nick Sheffield," she told him with feeling.

She made his heart swell, he thought, and she always would. "I love you, too, Georgie," he told her. And then he dropped a kiss on Emmie's head. "Both of you."

With a cry of joy, Georgie wrapped her arms around his neck just as Emmie wrapped herself around both of their lower torsos, hugging them for all she was worth.

Nick lowered his mouth to Georgie's. The kiss was long and emotional and promised to bind them together for the rest of their natural lives.

Epilogue

The rain came down, sliding along the surface of the headstones like tears heavy with grief.

Because of the inclement weather, the cemetery was empty, except for the one lone figure who stood before a grave site that had only the simplest of markers to designate where the woman known as Rebecca Totten was buried.

Rebecca had no family, no people who came forward to claim her. No one who came to see her simple wooden casket as it was lowered into the ground. An anonymous envelope containing cash had been sent to the morgue. The note inside, printed on a generic laser printer, said the money was to be used for her burial. It was the only thing that had kept her from meeting eternity in the county's potter's field.

"They're going to pay for this, Rebecca. I swear to

you, they're going to pay for this. Every last one of those Coltons is going to wish they were never born before I'm finished with them. And I'm going to get that Sheffield guy, too. He should be lying here, not you. Not you." The last words ended in a sob he barely suppressed.

The rain began to fall harder, lashing down on the slicker he wore over his deputy's uniform.

He was alone in his grief. And now, without Rebecca, he was alone in the world.

Because of *them*.

How could everything go so wrong so quickly? He'd finally met someone he could care about, someone he *did* care about for the first time in his life, and they were set to make a life together. The plan had been perfect. They were going to start fresh, both of them, a whole new life together, funded by that little shrew's money. Taking it from her hadn't troubled his conscience in the slightest. If anything, it was poetic justice.

Georgie Grady was a Colton. She *owed* him. They all did. But instead of he and Rebecca living happily ever after, now he was going to have to live unhappily ever after without her. All because of that bitch and that man she had staying with her.

Well, they were going to pay. They all were. Pay for his growing up without a father, pay for his growing old without Rebecca. Someway, somehow, he was going to get them all. Especially the Senator. Because it was his fault at bottom.

Adam swore it in his heart.

It gave him a reason to live.

* * * * *

Get a sneak peek of the next story in our exciting
THE COLTONS: FAMILY FIRST *miniseries.*
Turn the page to begin Beth Cornelison's
RANCHER'S REDEMPTION,
available from Silhouette Romantic Suspense
October 2008.

Chapter 1

He had a trespasser.

Clay Colton narrowed a wary gaze on the unfamiliar blue sedan parked under a stand of mesquite trees. This corner of the Bar None, Clay's horse ranch, was as flat as a beer left out in the Texas sun, and he'd spotted the car from half a mile away.

Tapping his dusty white Stetson back from his forehead, Clay wiped his sweaty brow. Finding a strange sedan on his property didn't sit well with him— especially in light of the recent trouble his sister, Georgie, had endured. He still got sick chills thinking how a woman had broken into his sister's home, stolen from her and passed herself off as Georgie.

A shiver crawled up Clay's spine despite the scorching June heat. Esperanza, Texas, his home for all his twenty-six years, had always been a safe place, no real crime to mention. He clicked his tongue and gave his work horse, Crockett, a little kick. His mount trotted forward, and as he neared the car, Clay saw that the Ford Taurus had crashed into one of the mesquites, crumpling the front fender. A fresh sense of alarm tripped through him.

"Hello? Anyone there?" Clay swung down from Crockett and cautiously approached the car. Visions of an injured, bleeding driver flashed through his mind and bumped his blood pressure higher. "Is anyone there?"

He peered into the driver's side window. Empty. The car had been abandoned.

Removing his hat, Clay raked sweaty black hair away from his eyes and circled to the back of the sedan. The trunk was ajar, and he glimpsed a white shopping sack inside. Using one finger to nudge open the trunk, Clay checked inside the bag.

His breath caught.

The bag was full of cash.

Intuition, combined with fresh memories of Georgie's recent brush with identity theft, tickled the nape of Clay's neck, making the fine hairs stand up. A wrecked and abandoned sedan with a bag of money meant trouble, no matter how you added it up. He stepped back and pulled his cell phone from the clip on his belt. He dialed his friend Sheriff Jericho Yates's number from memory.

"Jericho, it's Clay. I'm out on the southwest corner of my land near the ravine, and I've come across an abandoned Taurus. The car hit a mesquite and banged up the front end, but I don't see any sign of the driver."

Sheriff Yates grunted. "You don't see anyone around? Maybe the driver tried to walk out for help."

Clay scanned the area again, squinting against the bright June sun from under the rim of his Stetson. "Naw. Don't see anybody. But it gets better. There's a bag of money in the trunk. A lot of money. Large bundles of bills. Could be as much as a hundred grand."

He heard Jericho whistle his awe then sigh. "Listen, Clay. Don't touch anything. Until I determine otherwise you should consider the car and everything around it a crime scene. I'll be right out."

Clay thanked the sheriff and snapped his cell phone closed. He climbed back on Crockett and headed toward his original destination—the broken section of fence at the Black Creek ravine. Regardless of where the car and money came from and what the sheriff determined had happened to the driver, Clay had work to do, and the business of ranching waited on nothing.

Several minutes later, the rumble of car engines drew Clay's attention. He looked up from the barbed wire he'd strung and spotted Jericho's cruiser and a deputy's patrol car headed toward the abandoned Taurus. He laid down his wire cutters and shucked his work gloves. Grabbing a fence post for leverage, he climbed out of the steep ravine and strode across the hard, dry earth to meet the sheriff.

Jericho extended a hand in greeting. "Clay."

Shaking his friend's hand, Clay nodded a hello. "Afternoon, Jericho. So what did you learn about the car?"

Jericho sighed. "It's a rental from a little outfit up the road. Reported stolen a few days ago."

Clay arched a thick eyebrow. "Stolen?" He scowled. "Guess it figures. So now what?"

Jericho squinted in the bright sun and glanced toward the stolen Taurus where one of his deputies was already marking off the area with yellow police tape. "Chances are that money didn't come from someone's mattress. Heaven only knows what we could be dealing with here. I'll call in a crime scene team to do a thorough investigation. Probably San Antonio. They'd be closest."

A crime scene team.

The words resounded in Clay's ears like a gong, and he stiffened.

Tamara.

He worked to hide the shot of pain that swept over him as bittersweet memories swamped his brain.

Clay had two regrets in life. The first was his failure with Ryder—the brother he'd helped raise, the brother who'd gone astray and ended up in prison.

His second was his failed marriage. Five years ago, his high school sweetheart had walked away from their three-year marriage to follow her dream of becoming a crime scene investigator. Clay blamed himself for her leaving. If he'd been more sensitive to her needs, if he could have made her happier, if he could have found a way to—

"Clay, be sure to tell your men this area is off limits until we finish our investigation."

"Right."

"And we'll need you to answer some questions later."

Clay cut a sharp glance toward Sheriff Yates.

Jericho raised a hand to forestall Clay's protest. "Just basic stuff. You're not a suspect. All standard procedure."

Clay clenched his teeth. "Fine. Whatever you need." Removing his Stetson, Clay raked his fingers through his unkempt hair. Clay waved a hand. "I should get back to work."

Pulling his worn gloves from his back pocket, Clay

strode back toward the ravine where his fence had been damaged and got busy stringing wire again. He had a large section to repair before he went back to the house, and all the usual chores of a thriving ranch to finish before he called it a day. Unfortunately, although fixing the damaged fence was hot, hard work, it didn't require any particular mental concentration. So Clay's thoughts drifted—to the one person he'd spent the last five years trying to get out of his head.

His ex-wife.

If he knew Tamara, not only had she achieved her dream of working in investigative law enforcement, but she was also likely working for a large city department by now, moving up the ranks with her skill, gritty determination and sharp mind. Once Tamara set her sights on a goal, little could stand in her way of reaching it.

Except a misguided husband, who'd foolishly thought that ranching would be enough to fill her life and make her happy.

A prick of guilt twisted in Clay's gut.

He gave the barbed wire a vicious tug. His grip slipped, and the razor-sharp barb pierced his glove.

"Damn it!' he growled and flung off his glove to suck the blood beading on the pad of his thumb.

String wire might not take much mental power, but letting his mind rehash the painful dissolution of his marriage didn't serve any purpose. Tamara was gone, and no amount of regret or second guessing could change that. Besides, he was married to his ranch now. Keeping the Bar None running smoothly was a labor of love that took all his energy, all his time. He'd scraped and saved, sweated and toiled to build the Bar None from nothing but a boy's youthful dream.

But today the sense of accomplishment and pride that normally filled him when he surveyed his land or closed his financial books at the end of the day was shadowed by the reminder of what could have been.

Clay squinted up at the blazing Texas sun, which was far lower in the sky than he'd realized. How long had he been out here?

Flipping his wrist, he checked his watch. Two hours.

Crockett snorted and tossed his mane.

"Yeah, I know, boy. Almost done. I'm ready to get back to the stables and get something to drink too."

Like Jack Daniel's. Something to help take the edge off. Revived memories of Tamara left him off balance and had picked the scab from a wound he'd thought healed.

He snipped the wire he'd secured on the last post and started gathering his tools.

"Clay?"

At first he thought he'd imagined the soft feminine voice, an illusion conjured by thoughts of his ex-wife. But the voice called his name again.

He shielded his eyes from the sun's bright glare as he angled his gaze toward the top of the ravine. A slim, golden-haired beauty strode across the parched land and stopped at the edge of the rise. "Clay, can I talk to you?"

Clay's mouth went dry, and his heart did a Texas two-step. "Tamara?"

* * * * *

Turn the page for a sneak preview of
AFTERSHOCK, *a new anthology*
featuring New York Times *bestselling author*
Sharon Sala.

Available October 2008.

n●cturne™

Dramatic and sensual tales of paranormal romance.

Chapter 1

October
New York City

Nicole Masters was sitting cross-legged on her sofa while a cold autumn rain peppered the windows of her fourth-floor apartment. She was poking at the ice cream in her bowl and trying not to be in a mood.

Six weeks ago, a simple trip to her neighborhood pharmacy had turned into a nightmare. She'd walked into the middle of a robbery. She never even saw the man who shot her in the head and left her for dead. She'd survived, but some of her senses had not. She was dealing with short-term memory loss and a tendency to stagger. Even though she'd been told the problems were most likely temporary, she waged a daily battle with depression.

Her parents had been killed in a car wreck when she

was twenty-one. And except for a few friends—and most recently her boyfriend, Dominic Tucci, who lived in the apartment right above hers, she was alone. Her doctor kept reminding her that she should be grateful to be alive, and on one level she knew he was right. But he wasn't living in her shoes.

If she'd been anywhere else but at that pharmacy when the robbery happened, she wouldn't have died twice on the way to the hospital. Instead of being grateful that she'd survived, she couldn't stop thinking of what she'd lost.

But that wasn't the end of her troubles. On top of everything else, something strange was happening inside her head. She'd begun to hear odd things: sounds, not voices—at least, she didn't think it was voices. It was more like the distant noise of rapids—a rush of wind and water inside her head that, when it came, blocked out everything around her. It didn't happen often, but when it did, it was frightening, and it was driving her crazy.

The blank moments, which is what she called them, even had a rhythm. First there came that sound, then a cold sweat, then panic with no reason. Part of her feared it was the beginning of an emotional breakdown. And part of her feared it wasn't—that it was going to turn out to be a permanent souvenir of her resurrection.

Frustrated with herself and the situation as it stood, she upped the sound on the TV remote. But instead of *Wheel of Fortune,* an announcer broke in with a special bulletin.

"This just in. Police are on the scene of a kidnapping that occurred only hours ago at The Dakota. Molly Dane, the six-year-old daughter of one of Hollywood's blockbuster stars, Lyla Dane, was taken by force from the family apartment. At this time they have yet to receive a ransom demand. The housekeeper was seriously injured during the abduction, and is, at the present time, in surgery. Police are hoping to be able to talk to her once she regains consciousness. In the meantime, we are going now to a press conference with Lyla Dane."

Horrified, Nicole stilled as the cameras went live to where the actress was speaking before a bank of microphones. The shock and terror in Lyla Dane's voice were physically painful to watch. But even though Nicole kept upping the volume, the sound continued to fade.

Just when she was beginning to think something was wrong with her set, the broadcast suddenly switched from the Dane press conference to what appeared to be footage of the kidnapping, beginning with footage from inside the apartment.

When the front door suddenly flew back against the wall and four men rushed in, Nicole gasped. Horrified, she quickly realized that this must have been caught on a security camera inside the Dane apartment.

As Nicole continued to watch, a small Asian woman, who she guessed was the maid, rushed forward in an effort to keep them out. When one of the men hit her in the face with his gun, Nicole moaned. The violence was too reminiscent of what she'd lived through. Sick to her stomach, she fisted her hands against her belly, wishing it was over, but unable to tear her gaze away.

When the maid dropped to the carpet, the same man followed with a vicious kick to the little woman's midsection that lifted her off the floor.

"Oh, my God," Nicole said. When blood began to pool beneath the maid's head, she started to cry.

As the tape played on, the four men split up in different directions. The camera caught one running down a long marble hallway, then disappearing into a room. Moments later he reappeared, carrying a little girl, who Nicole assumed was Molly Dane. The child was wearing a pair of red pants and a white turtleneck sweater, and her hair was partially blocking her abductor's face as he carried her down the hall. She was kicking and screaming in his arms, and when he slapped her, it elicited an agonized scream that brought the other three running. Nicole watched in horror as one of them ran up and put his hand over Molly's face. Seconds later, she went limp.

One moment they were in the foyer, then they were gone.

Nicole jumped to her feet, then staggered drunkenly. The bowl of ice cream she'd absentmindedly placed in her lap shattered at her feet, splattering glass and melting ice cream everywhere.

The picture on the screen abruptly switched from the kidnapping to what Nicole assumed was a rerun of Lyla Dane's plea for her daughter's safe return, but she was numb.

Before she could think what to do next, the doorbell rang. Startled by the unexpected sound, she shakily swiped at the tears and took a step forward. She didn't feel the glass shards piercing her feet until she took the second step. At that point, sharp pains shot through her foot. She gasped, then looked down in confusion. Her legs looked as if she'd been running through mud, and she was standing in broken glass and ice cream, while a thin ribbon of blood seeped out from beneath her toes.

"Oh, no," Nicole mumbled, then stifled a second moan of pain.

The doorbell rang again. She shivered, then clutched her head in confusion.

"Just a minute!" she yelled, then tried to sidestep the rest of the debris as she hobbled to the door.

When she looked through the peephole in the door, she didn't know whether to be relieved or regretful.

It was Dominic, and as usual, she was a mess.

Nicole smiled a little self-consciously as she opened the door to let him in. "I just don't know what's happening to me. I think I'm losing my mind."

"Hey, don't talk about my woman like that."

Nicole rode the surge of delight his words brought. "So I'm still your woman?"

Dominic lowered his head.

Their lips met.

The kiss proceeded.

Slowly.

Thoroughly.

* * * * *

Be sure to look for the
AFTERSHOCK *anthology next month, as
well as other exciting paranormal stories
from Silhouette Nocturne.
Available in October wherever books are sold.*

nocturne™

NEW YORK TIMES BESTSELLING AUTHOR

SHARON SALA

JANIS REAMES HUDSON
DEBRA COWAN

AFTERSHOCK

Three women are brought to the brink of death...
only to discover the aftershock of their trauma has
left them with unexpected and unwelcome gifts of
paranormal powers. Now each woman must learn to
accept her newfound abilities while fighting for life,
love and second chances....

Available October wherever books are sold.

Romantic
SUSPENSE

**Sparked by Danger,
Fueled by Passion.**

USA TODAY bestselling author

Merline Lovelace

Undercover Wife

Secret agent Mike Callahan, code name Hawkeye,
objects when he's paired with sophisticated
Gillian Ridgeway on a dangerous spy mission
to Hong Kong. Gillian has secretly been in love
with him for years, but Hawk is an overprotective
man with a wounded past that threatens to
resurface. Now the two must put their lives—
and hearts—at risk for each other.

Available October wherever books are sold.

REQUEST YOUR FREE BOOKS!

2 FREE NOVELS PLUS 2 FREE GIFTS!

Silhouette® Romantic

SUSPENSE

Sparked by Danger, Fueled by Passion!

YES! Please send me 2 FREE Silhouette® Romantic Suspense novels and my 2 FREE gifts (gifts are worth about $10). After receiving them, if I don't wish to receive any more books, I can return the shipping statement marked "cancel." If I don't cancel, I will receive 4 brand-new novels every month and be billed just $4.24 per book in the U.S. or $4.99 per book in Canada, plus 25¢ shipping and handling per book plus applicable taxes, if any*. That's a savings of at least 15% off the cover price! I understand that accepting the 2 free books and gifts places me under no obligation to buy anything. I can always return a shipment and cancel at any time. Even if I never buy another book from Silhouette, the two free books and gifts are mine to keep forever.

240 SDN EEX6   340 SDN EEYJ

Name	(PLEASE PRINT)

Address		Apt. #

City	State/Prov.	Zip/Postal Code

Signature (if under 18, a parent or guardian must sign)

Mail to the **Silhouette Reader Service:**

IN U.S.A.: P.O. Box 1867, Buffalo, NY 14240-1867
IN CANADA: P.O. Box 609, Fort Erie, Ontario L2A 5X3

Not valid to current subscribers of Silhouette Romantic Suspense books.

Want to try two free books from another line?
Call 1-800-873-8635 or visit www.morefreebooks.com.

* Terms and prices subject to change without notice. N.Y. residents add applicable sales tax. Canadian residents will be charged applicable provincial taxes and GST. Offer not valid in Quebec. This offer is limited to one order per household. All orders subject to approval. Credit or debit balances in a customer's account(s) may be offset by any other outstanding balance owed by or to the customer. Please allow 4 to 6 weeks for delivery. Offer available while quantities last.

Your Privacy: Silhouette is committed to protecting your privacy. Our Privacy Policy is available online at www.eHarlequin.com or upon request from the Reader Service. From time to time we make our lists of customers available to reputable third parties who may have a product or service of interest to you. If you would prefer we not share your name and address, please check here. ☐

SRS08R

Silhouette®
Romantic
SUSPENSE

COMING NEXT MONTH

#1531 UNDERCOVER WIFE—Merline Lovelace
Code Name: Danger
Rough around the edges Mike Callahan, code name Hawkeye, objects when he's paired with sophisticated Gillian Ridgeway on a dangerous spy mission to Hong Kong. Hawk is an overprotective man with a wounded past, and Gillian has secretly been in love with him for years. Now the two must put their lives—and hearts—at risk for each other.

#1532 RANCHER'S REDEMPTION—Beth Cornelison
The Coltons: Family First
Rancher Clay Colton discovers a wrecked car and a bag of money on his property, so the local police call in a CSI team—headed by his ex-wife, Tamara. As she investigates, the two are thrown into the path of danger, uncovering secrets about the crime as well as their true feelings for each other.

#1533 TERMS OF SURRENDER—Kylie Brant
Alpha Squad
Targeted by a bank robber bent on revenge, hostage negotiators and former lovers Dace Recker and Jolie Conrad are reunited against their will. The FBI has recruited them to draw out the killer, but their close proximity to each other will draw out wounds from their past. Can they heal their hearts for a second chance at love?

#1534 THE DOCTOR'S MISSION—Lyn Stone
Special Ops
When Dr. Nick Sandro is recruited to help COMPASS agent Cate Olin recover after a head injury, his mission is complicated by the feelings they still harbor for each other. Escaping to Tuscany as a terrorist sends men after Cate, Nick must do all he can to protect her. But they'll have to work together to destroy the final threat.

SRSCNM0908